DARKNESS

COMMON LAW BOOK THREE

Kate Sherwood

RIPTIDE
PUBLISHING

Riptide Publishing
PO Box 1537
Burnsville, NC 28714
www.riptidepublishing.com

Darkness
Copyright © 2017 by Kate Sherwood

Cover art: Natasha Snow, natashasnowdesigns.com
Editor: Carole-ann Galloway
Layout: L.C. Chase, lcchase.com/design.htm

ISBN: 978-1-62649-532-6

First edition
March, 2017

Also available in ebook:
ISBN: 978-1-62649-531-9

DARKNESS

COMMON LAW BOOK THREE

Kate Sherwood

RIPTIDE
PUBLISHING

TABLE OF

CONTENTS

CHAPTER 1

Jericho Crewe was at home, pretending to watch TV while brooding about the sorry state of his life, when the phone rang. Nikki's tone. He was tempted to ignore it, but she was his father's widow, the mother of his two half siblings—his responsibility. So he answered, expecting to hear her strident demands for whatever favor she'd managed to dream up.

Instead he heard, "I like snakes," in a childish voice.

"Elijah? That you? You like snakes?" Jericho took a moment to clue in. "Oh, okay. Our deal. Snakes instead of guns."

"Guns are still best, but you said I should tell you what I like second best. That's snakes."

It had taken the kid a couple months to come up with it, but Jericho supposed it was better late than never. "Okay. Good." He tried to think it through. "I like snakes too. Maybe we should go for a hike and see if we can find some? Or maybe the zoo . . . there's a little zoo down in Billings, I think, and I could check if they have snakes."

"Mom says they do. She says it has to be an overnight trip if we go to Billings, because it's far. She says Nicolette has to come too, and you have to find something Nicolette wants to do on the trip so she's not left out."

Yup, that sounded like Nikki. Why impose on him for one child's care when she could push for two? Of course, free babysitting was the least sinister explanation for the woman's sudden interest in having Jericho spend time with the kids. "Uh . . . did she have any idea what Nicolette would want to do?"

"She said this whole thing is your plan, so it's your problem to figure that out."

Of course it was. Jericho thought about having both kids in the car with him for about four hours each way, staying in a hotel with them, trying to keep them from setting the place on fire or freeing all the animals at the zoo—"How about we find something closer to home? Hey, does Nicolette like horses? We could go horseback riding somewhere there's likely to be snakes."

"I don't want to ride a horse."

Of course he didn't.

"Uncle Wade says you should talk to Cory Barker about snakes. He says Cory has lots."

Jericho tried not to react to Wade's name. It had been a couple months since their last meeting, up in the forest. Which was good. Jericho's life would be a hell of a lot easier if he could stay the hell away from Wade Granger. Not feel snubbed by the man's absence. Not feel the aching need in his gut expanding from a tiny acorn into what sometimes felt like a full-grown oak tree. Wasn't lying awake at night, imagining Wade's hands on his body instead of his own. Not at all. "I'm not sure I know Cory Barker."

"Uncle Wade says you should get to know him."

Maybe Uncle Wade should take you to see Cory Barker and his damn snakes. Maybe Uncle Wade should mind his own damn business and stop telling me what to do. Maybe Uncle Wade should shove one of Cory Barker's snakes right—

"Are you going to call him? You said you'd get me something for my second-favorite thing. That's what you said."

"Yeah, I'll— I don't know about Cory Barker, but I'll figure it out, for sure. Maybe not Cory Barker, but . . . snakes. You got it. And what about your sister? Has she got a favorite thing yet?"

"It's not fair that she gets her first favorite and I only get my second favorite."

"If her first favorite is lethal, she's not going to get it, either. Is she there? Can I talk to her?"

"She's busy. Bye."

And Jericho was left staring at his phone. What the hell was Wade up to? Was he just being helpful, suggesting a way to give Elijah a treat without too much trouble? Maybe, but Wade was rarely *just* anything.

Jericho hit one of the stored numbers in his phone, and a moment later heard, "Mosely Sheriff's Department. Deputy Garron speaking."

"It's Jericho. Do you know anything about a guy named Cory Barker?"

"Cory Barker? Sure, we've had him in a few times. General lowlife, nothing too exciting. Why?"

"Don't suppose you know if he keeps snakes?"

A disgusted snort. "Wouldn't surprise me."

"Is there—" Damn, how to word this? "Is there a reason we'd be interested in him for anything going on lately?"

Jericho could practically hear Garron's scowl. "What's this about?"

Jericho wasn't going to share that detail. He wasn't going to admit that his ex-lover had possibly given him a tip, but had equally possibly just been helping him find snakes for an annoying six-year-old. He wasn't going to explain that even if it did turn out to be a tip, there was a damn good chance it was based on furthering Wade's interests rather than those of the sheriff's department. There was no way to explain any of it. No way to explain Wade. And also no way to ignore him, not for Jericho. "Have you got a phone number or an address for him? Cory Barker?"

"Hang on," Garron grumbled. He was back a minute later. "No phone number. As I recall, there was lots of swearing about us not having his permission to call. I've got an address, though. Over by the elementary school, Seventeen Thompson Crescent."

"Thanks."

"You going over there? You need backup?"

"No." At least, he hoped he didn't. "It's not a police issue. I'm just—I'm looking for snakes."

"Right," Garron drawled. "Good luck with that."

So Jericho hauled himself off the couch and headed out to his old Mustang. It was a nice night, with no clouds and a warm summer breeze, and it would have made more sense to go find a park and look up at the stars. Instead, he was chasing down a snake lead, half hoping it was also something else.

He pulled up in front of a modest, ragged bungalow. The town had lost population since the mine closed, and it was cheaper to rent houses than apartments most of the time. But there wasn't a lot of money spent on maintaining the near-worthless rental houses, that was for sure.

He noted the battered pickup in the driveway, and headed for the front door. All the windows of the house were closed, and he peered around the side, trying to spot an air conditioning unit. Didn't see one. So the closed windows were suspicious. But maybe the house was just naturally cool. And it wasn't like the night was that hot.

All the neighbors had their windows open, though. Jericho approached the front door with a little extra caution. He knocked. Gentle, polite, just a member of the community making a somewhat strange inquiry about snakes. His Glock was reassuringly solid in his waistband holster, and the fact that he'd worn it, the fact that he was thinking about it—his subconscious was telling him something, and he'd better listen to it.

Another knock, this one more forceful, and he heard movement inside the house. Someone stumbled over something, banged into the door. "Who is it?"

"My name's Jay," Jericho said. *Ask about the snakes, get away from here, go home.* But he couldn't do it. "I heard maybe you could help me out." *Okay, that was still vague. You don't have to go through with this.*

Then the door opened a crack, and a whiff of stale air escaped. Stale, chemical-laden air. Jericho wished he didn't recognize that smell, but he did. Jesus Christ, this asshole was cooking meth in a residential neighborhood, four doors down from the elementary school. What would the blast radius be if the place went up—just how much damage would be done? It would depend on the time of day. If they got lucky, the explosion would only take out this house and probably one on either side. But if the timing was wrong, and kids were walking by on their way to school—

"Who told you to come here?" the man inside demanded. It was hard to see him clearly, but he looked like he was in his midtwenties, too damn thin, and too damn jumpy. He kept wiping his nose with the back of his hand, and Jericho could see raw spots on both the hand and the nose.

"Guy down at the bar—shit, I forget his name." Jericho had never worked narcotics, but even he knew this was not a great cover story. Somehow, though, he thought it might work on what was clearly an amateur setup and a clown who was obviously tweaking. "Midsize guy, kinda skinny, with brown hair? He said you could hook me up." Jericho reached for his wallet. "What can you give me for eighty bucks?"

A moment of indecision, then greed took over. "A gram for ninety."

"Ninety? That's steep."

"That's the fucking price," the guy snarled, rubbing at his nose harder.

Jericho pretended to be indecisive. "Fine," he finally said, and opened his wallet. He held it carefully to be sure his police ID didn't show.

And that was when his phone rang. He ignored it, and held the bills out toward the tweaker, then snatched them back before they could be taken. "Where's the crank?"

"You don't trust me?"

"Let me see it."

Jericho's phone had stopped ringing, but then it started again, and it was obviously setting off the tweaker's nerves. "Aren't you going to answer that?"

"No. It's probably the bitch I'm buying this for. She's getting kinda . . . impatient."

That was when there was a loud thud behind him. He stepped to the side, trying to keep his eyes on the tweaker at the same time as he checked out the new disturbance. There were no streetlights, but Jericho could see a man by his car—had he just bashed his fist into the roof of Jericho's Mustang? "Hey," Jericho called. "You got a problem?"

"Yeah," came the response. "You're my fucking problem."

Jericho recognized the voice. *Shit. Shit, shit, shit.*

"You want this or not?" the tweaker demanded, holding a baggie out in Jericho's direction.

Jericho needed to change tack. "Who's that guy?" Jericho asked. "The guy by my car. What the hell's going on?"

"What? Fuck, I don't know him! He sounds like he knows you!"

"Fuck off!" Jericho called toward the street.

"Make me!"

"What, is he your buddy?" Jericho demanded of the tweaker. "I give you the cash, and I go down there, and he steals the crank? Fuck you, man!"

"I don't fucking know him!"

"Bullshit!" Jericho lunged forward, but did it slowly enough that the tweaker could get the door shut and locked. "Asshole!" Jericho yelled, and kicked the door for good measure.

He made sure his shirt was covering his holstered gun, then turned and stomped down the stairs and out to the street.

"He's cooking meth right next to a school," he growled as soon as he was close enough for Special Agent Hockley to hear him. "The DEA's just *sitting* on that?"

"We're on it," Hockley responded, his voice also low and intense. "We've got a special team coming in to make sure it's taken apart cleanly. We're quietly evacuating the neighbors. We're doing this *right*, Crewe, and we do not need you wandering in and making a mess of everything. Get the hell out of here. And answer your phone next time!"

"Goddamn it," Jericho said, mostly to himself. "I only wanted to find some fucking snakes."

CHAPTER 2

"**W**hy the fuck did Wade Granger want to mess up our bust?" Hockley demanded the next morning. He was wearing the proof of his long night in the stubble on his face and the bags under his eyes, but apparently his energy was undiminished. "Why would he send you into a situation like that?"

Jericho wanted to argue with the "send you" part of that question, but he wasn't sure what he could say. It had taken about ten words from Wade, not even spoken directly to Jericho, to have him running across town to the door in question. He leaned back in his creaky leather desk chair and watched the irate federal agent pacing around his office. "I suppose it's possible he was helping me find some snakes."

"The snake thing is just weird. Why the hell does the kid want to see snakes?"

"Maybe because Wade planted the idea in his head to get me to go mess up your bust. Maybe because snakes are cool. I truly don't know." Jericho sighed. "It's possible Wade wasn't aware of your operation. I mean, if you've plugged the pipeline through Kayla's dad, he might not be as clear on what you guys are up to. And if that's the case— it's honestly not impossible that he wanted to draw my attention to the fact that someone was cooking meth four doors down from an elementary school. Summer vacation's almost over, and if that place had blown up when kids were walking by, it could have been a disaster. It's a damn good thing you got it cleaned up last night. And Wade's helped before, when protecting kids was involved."

"Was his previous assistance about protecting kids or protecting *you*?" Hockley shook his head. "It's a fucked-up situation, Jericho. You know that."

Jericho couldn't deny it. And in a way, as much as the DEA's continued presence in Mosely was a nuisance, he knew things would get even more fucked-up when—or if—they ever decided their work in the area was done. As it was, Jericho was mostly busy helping Kayla run the department and enforcing the simpler laws that affected a rural community. Large-scale investigations of people like Wade Granger? He could ignore them, as long as the feds were around to do that work. Without the feds, whatever was going on between Jericho and Wade would boil up a hell of a lot faster.

The not-entirely-unpleasant churning in his gut that came when he thought about heating up with Wade was a sign that he still needed to get his head in the right place about that relationship. Damn it. "He's attached himself to Nikki's life. Her kids. I could ignore her— I'd be *happy* to ignore her—if she were on her own. But I feel like I've got some obligation to the kids, you know? They're my half siblings. And that means I'm going to keep having contact with Wade, even if it's as indirect as this was."

Hockley grimaced, then said, "There's something else you should know."

There had probably never been *good* news presented with a lead-in like that, so Jericho braced himself and waited.

"You know we've been questioning the bikers," Hockley said. Most of the major players from the recent bust were being held without bail, and the feds had been going through their typical investigations. Nothing to worry Jericho about that. Hockley paused a moment, then clearly decided he had to go on. "We're casting a wide net. Asking questions about the specific crimes that they've already been charged with, but also about larger issues and crimes we suspect they were involved in."

"Okay . . ."

"We've been asking them about your father's death. The questions haven't been too targeted, since we haven't really got that much to go on. But we've been asking."

Jericho just nodded. As always when his father was mentioned, there was no use trying to catalog, much less understand, the emotions that raced through him.

"We haven't gotten much. But a couple days ago we were talking to Mike DeMonte, and he said . . ." Hockley peered down at his phone, apparently reading a note word-for-word. "He said we should 'tell Junior to look closer to home on that one.'"

"'Closer to home.'" Jericho tried to ignore the twisting in his gut, tried to treat the response like an intellectual problem. What sort of information would the bikers have about his father's death? Who might they have heard from? And who would they consider close to Jericho's home? "You're thinking he meant Wade?"

"Seems like a logical assumption. Granger's the one who's benefited most from your father's death, after all. His recent business growth has been based almost exclusively on activating the contacts and other information from that thumb drive."

Jericho nodded dully. Wade had benefited. Wade was capable of killing a man. Wade had pulled a gun on Jericho himself fairly recently. Wade was a reasonable suspect. God, what did it mean that Jericho was working so hard to forget that?

His phone rang then with Kayla's distinctive tone, and he tried not to look too pathetically grateful for the distraction as he answered the call.

"We've got a body," Kayla said. "Over on Forest Lane, those rental houses. White female, midforties, suspected homicide. You've got the experience on that, so I want you to take lead."

Jericho sat up a little straighter. He was aware of Hockley listening, but didn't temper his words. "You think it's actually ours? The feds aren't going to sweep in and take over?" He glanced over at Hockley, who just raised a sardonic eyebrow.

"We are not currently aware of any reason for the feds to be involved," Kayla said.

Jericho was already standing when he jerked his head in a sort of good-bye to Hockley. He started for the door, phone still clapped to his ear. "You got an address for me?"

"I'm coming over with you. You're the lead, but I'm part of this. Meet me downstairs."

"Yes, ma'am."

He wasn't *happy* that a woman was dead, he told himself as he jogged down the stairs, leaving Hockley behind. No, not happy she was dead, and not even happy he was heading off to investigate her death. It wasn't happiness he was feeling, just a sense of purpose. Everything had been too complicated lately, first with his father, then with the feds, and always, of course, with Wade. But this sounded straightforward. A woman had been alive, and now she was dead, and there was reason to believe her change in status wasn't due to natural causes. Jericho would find out who had killed her, and why, and he'd gather evidence to ensure that the right person was punished. Everything would make sense. He hoped.

"Please tell me Wade Granger wasn't the one who found the body," he said as Kayla fell in beside him and they charged out the door.

She gave him a startled look. "Do you have some reason to believe he's involved?"

"No. Just, you know—just my horrific luck."

"Jay, if you're investigating drug trafficking and semi-organized crime in Mosely, Montana, it's not *bad luck* that leads to you repeatedly encountering Wade Granger."

Well, she had a point there, but it wasn't one he wanted to think about too hard. "So who did find her?" he asked, then hesitated as the sidewalk ended at the asphalt of the parking lot.

"I'll drive," Kayla said, and they strode toward her cruiser. "We got the call from Ned Appleby, the owner of the hardware store. You used to work there, right? In high school? So you know Ned."

"Mr. Appleby." The man had given Jericho a chance when no one else would, and he'd repay the favor by using the proper honorifics. "How'd he get involved? Do we have an ID on the victim?"

"Not firm yet, but we think it's Lorraine Mackey. Body's in her house, and the general description matches. Ned didn't get too close to her, understandably." She climbed into the driver's seat, and Jericho took shotgun.

Lorraine Mackey. Damn, it was always harder when the victim was someone he'd seen living and breathing and walking around. Lorraine had been a known prostitute, an alcoholic and addict more likely to stumble than walk—Jericho had written her up for public inebriation twice in his short time in Mosely—but she'd at least been alive. And now someone had made her dead, on his watch.

"Dangerous line of work," he said once he and Kayla were both buckled in. "Did she let johns into the house?"

"Yeah." Kayla shook her head. "Hell, we practically chased her into doing it. We'd bust her for solicitation if she was working the streets, but we always figured whatever she did inside her own home was her own business."

He was familiar with that way of thinking, but it was easier to recognize its destructiveness in someone else. "Kayla." He waited until she looked over at him. "Let's hold off until we find out what happened. We've got plenty of time to feel guilty about shit then, okay?"

"Okay," she agreed reluctantly. "I thought I could get a head start. That's all."

"I appreciate your commitment to efficiency."

"On the plus side," she said as she pulled out of the parking spot, "Wade Granger doesn't run whores. I've never known whether that was out of respect for his mother or simply a personal preference, but this might actually be a truly independent crime. No Wade, no feds. No complications."

"That is a plus."

They drove the rest of the way to Lorraine's house in silence.

CHAPTER 3

J ericho stayed at the crime scene long enough to get a general impression and to make sure it was properly secured, ready for the lab guys to arrive. He toured the property and noticed with a sinking feeling how heavily treed the backyard was and how hard the dirt in the alley behind the house was. There'd be no tire tracks to find, and the other side of the alley was deep forest, not more houses. There was a rough path leading into the woods, and at some point he'd have to follow it and figure out where it ended. But the significant thing right then was that this was an easy house to approach without being seen. The chances of an eyewitness were low. Still, he checked that the deputies had a good list of questions to ask on their initial survey of the neighbors and then found Kayla and suggested they get the hell back to the station.

"So, you're squeamish?" Kay asked as she drove. She didn't sound disapproving, exactly. More amused.

"No. But I saw what I had to see, and the crime scene guys can do the rest."

"You didn't want to soak up the vibe?" He wasn't sure if she was genuinely curious about his methods or was prompting him to do things the way she wanted.

"I absolutely want to. I want to soak up the vibe with the scene as it was at the time of the murder. The way it is now, with a bunch of nervous, nosy deputies? Neighbors pushing against the yellow tape and flies starting to buzz? That's not useful to me. It interferes."

Kayla was silent for a while before she said, "Your captain in LA told me you've got the makings of a topflight homicide cop. She thought you were going to burn out too early to make an impact, though."

Jericho wasn't sure what to say to that, so he defaulted to smart-ass. "Well, after my relaxing vacation here in Mosely, I'm sure my inevitable burnout can be significantly delayed."

"She told me she doubted you'd come back to LA," Kayla said, still calmly watching the road as she drove. "According to her, you always seemed like a visitor, not a resident."

"Well, I've met that woman about three times in my life, so I'm not convinced she really knows what the fuck she's talking about."

"Is she wrong?"

"About me being a burnout in waiting? I'd like to think so, yeah."

"So you see yourself taking it to retirement with the LAPD? I mean, after your lovely Mosely vacation, of course."

"You don't think I'm going to stick around up here, do you? I mean, so far I've been accused of corruption, dragged into undercover work I wasn't prepared for, suspended, and when all that wasn't happening, bored to death. There doesn't seem to be a promising future for me with the Mosely Sheriff's Department."

"You forgot about getting shot."

"Technically, that happened before you hired me. I'm giving you a pass on that one."

They pulled into the department parking lot then, and neither of them said anything as they climbed out of the car.

"I'm not saying you're going to stick around here," Kayla said just before they reached the double glass doors at the front of the building. "But I don't see you going back to LA."

Shit. Neither do I. He'd never made a conscious decision about it, but somehow his life on the coast had started receding from his mind, and now it was so far away it was hard to even remember it. "Jesus, Kay, do we need to get into this right now? We've got a woman who was clearly murdered, a truly messed-up crime scene, and a chance to actually fucking do something about it instead of sitting back and watching the feds screw things up. What d'ya say: can we just solve some crime instead of having a goddamn therapy session?"

Kayla raised an eyebrow, then lifted one hand flat in the air and pretended to write on it with the other. "Patient displays strong aversion to discussion of future."

"Patient prefers to focus on the present so he can figure out who the hell brutally murdered Lorraine Mackey," he responded, and immediately felt guilty when Kayla recoiled. She'd been playing, dealing with the trauma of the situation in her own way, just like all cops did. And he'd shamed her for it. "Of course, patient is a known asshole," he tried, and she was generous enough to smile at him.

They climbed the stairs and found Mr. Appleby waiting in one of the interview rooms, his hands wrapped around a mug of coffee as if he were trying to draw warmth from it. Jericho saw the man's lips moving and realized he was praying. *Shit.* Looking for forgiveness, or something else?

Jericho turned to Kayla. "Let me talk to him alone first, okay? You can listen in from the observation room, but let me talk to him first."

"Why?"

"Because Lorraine Mackey was an alcoholic, antisocial prostitute. I have no idea why Mr. Appleby was at her house, but I'm pretty sure he wasn't borrowing a cup of sugar." It wasn't something Jericho wanted to spend a lot of time thinking about, but that was true of just about every situation he encountered in the course of his work. "If he was there for the standard reason men visit Lorraine, he might be more comfortable telling me about it than you."

She didn't seem impressed, but she nodded reluctantly and headed down the hall that would lead to the observation room. Jericho pushed the interview room door open, and Mr. Appleby stood up so quickly he sloshed coffee onto his khaki trousers. He didn't even look down.

"My God, Jericho, this is a terrible thing." Usually, Mr. Appleby appeared younger than his age would suggest, but at that moment in the interview room Jericho could see the marks left by every year.

"It is." Jericho turned to shut the door behind him and tried to find the gentler version of his professional voice. "I need to ask you some questions about it. There's a camera set up behind the glass, there, and we'll be making an audio recording as well. This is for your protection, and for our use in investigating the crime. Do you understand?"

Mr. Appleby seemed taken aback. He'd clearly been expecting a bit of commiseration before they got down to business, but Jericho couldn't let himself think of Mr. Appleby as a friend, or as someone to whom he owed favors. Right then, the man was the sole witness in a homicide investigation. That was all.

Still, Jericho tried to smile a little as he gestured to the chair Mr. Appleby had abandoned. "Please, sit down." He hit the buttons to start the recording instruments and couldn't think of any other ways to delay. "Can you tell me what brought you to Ms. Mackey's house today?"

Mr. Appleby sat, then nodded shakily. "I— He's a good boy, Jericho. A good man. I know he's not the same as he was before the accident, I know there've been some problems, but something like this? No. I won't believe it."

A good boy. A good man, not the same . . . "Will Archer? Is that who you're talking about?"

"He came in to work this morning, about an hour late, and he was terribly upset. Couldn't say what the problem was, but he was—he was crying, couldn't sit still, he looked like he hadn't slept. Wasn't shaven, and he's always so particular about that. And there were—" Mr. Appleby stopped, swallowed, and continued in a smaller voice. "There were stains on his clothes. I couldn't be sure of the color because the fabric was dark. But under his nails it seemed brown."

"You suspected it was blood?"

"I called Mary to come help me with him, and we tried to check him over. We thought it was *his* blood, thought he'd been hurt. But he kept pushing us away. And we noticed there were no tears to his clothes, no sign of injury. So finally I asked him if someone else was hurt, and he nodded, in his way, and I said he had to take me to them. And he did."

"Where did he take you, Mr. Appleby?"

"Out through the back door. Down the alley, and then down a couple blocks. Then into the house. And that's where I saw her."

There were more questions that needed to be asked, details to be worked out. But first, Jericho had to take care of the essentials. "Where is Will now?"

"I don't know," Mr. Appleby whispered. "He made it through the kitchen, but refused to go any farther. I went on in—I was calling out as I went, truly hoping someone would answer me and demand to know what I was doing in their home—and found . . . what I found. Then I ran back to the kitchen to call the police, but Will was already gone by the time I got there."

Jericho knew Kayla was listening, knew she'd put out the APB. So he asked the rest of the questions he needed to ask. He did his job, trying not to think about the repercussions. He had to focus on the victim. Lorraine had been damaged by life, struggling to get by, but she'd been surviving. She hadn't wanted to die.

And just because Will had been at the scene it didn't mean he'd committed the crime. Not by a long shot. They'd find him, and then Jericho would have to work out some way to question him. They'd need medical records, psychiatric reports, interviews with the man's friends and neighbors. Crime scene analysis, witnesses from the community, evidence gathered through a variety of tools.

"We'll find him," Jericho promised Mr. Appleby. "And we'll do a thorough investigation. We'll work out what happened."

By the time the old man stood to leave, his color was better and he didn't look quite as shaky as he had before. Jericho walked him out and arranged for a car to take him back to the hardware store. The niceties were observed as if there wasn't a corpse a few blocks away, wasn't a murderer running free. Jericho had the discipline to keep an open mind, and he honestly hoped he'd find evidence to cast suspicion *away* from Will Archer. But he'd investigated a lot of murders, and they were rarely all that complicated, once you got the basics figured out. When there was an obvious suspect, that was usually the person who'd committed the crime.

It didn't matter that Will was one of Mr. Appleby's protégés, just as Jericho had been. Didn't matter that he'd gone to school with Jericho and always seemed like a good guy. Didn't matter that the accident that had injured his brain hadn't been his fault. If he'd done this to Lorraine, he would have to be caught and punished. The town would have to be protected. That was Jericho's job, and he would do it, no matter what.

CHAPTER 4

J ericho was back at the crime scene that afternoon, with the body gone and caution tape on all the doors, when he got the call from dispatch. A man had jumped out of the forest just a few blocks down from the scene, scared a couple of girls who'd been playing in the alley, and then had run back into the woods. The description wasn't great, but it was close enough for Jericho to call the hardware store as he drove to the spot where the man had been seen.

"It might not be Will," Jericho told Mr. Appleby. "And even if it is him, we may not be able to let you get close. Our priority will be your safety. But if it is him, and if he's calm enough to pay attention, hearing a familiar voice and seeing a friendly face may help us bring him in peacefully."

"I'm on my way out the door," Mr. Appleby promised.

Jericho arrived to find the two girls, maybe ten or twelve years old, huddled close to a man he assumed was their father. "They don't need to be here for this," Jericho told the man. "If you've given your information to the deputy, you should probably head out. We can take it from here."

"They were badly frightened," the man said. "I think they need closure. They need to see it was just a sad, pathetic excuse for a man, not a monster from the woods."

Jericho didn't have time to argue, and it wasn't like he was some sort of parenting expert anyway. "Stay behind the cars, then."

A few deputies had already been sent into the trees to circle around behind where they hoped the man was hiding, and Jericho approached the edge of the forest with caution. He could see the bent branches, the scuffed ground, and didn't have much trouble tracking what had clearly been a panicked flight rather than a disciplined retreat. Why had the man jumped out in the first place if he'd been so easily frightened away?

Jericho was about thirty feet into the forest, two deputies following close behind, when he saw the bright eyes staring at him from under a shrub. He lifted a hand to stop the deputies and slowly crouched to get a better look.

"Will," he said gently. There were scratches on Will's face, damage that could have been caused by tree branches—or by the fingernails of a woman desperately fighting for her life. "Hey, Will. I don't know if you remember me. Jericho Crewe? We went to school together, but that was a long time ago." Did Will have any memories from before the accident? Jericho had dropped by Will's apartment with a deputy, checking to see if the suspect had made it home, and found a tidy, Spartan space with no personal touches whatsoever. No signs of who Will was or what he cared about.

But a record check had shown several violent incidents in his past. Times when he'd gotten scared or angry, or more likely some toxic combination of the two, and lost control of himself. That matched what Jericho had seen at the crime scene. He'd have to wait for the coroner's report to be sure, but it looked like Lorraine had been beaten and then strangled. A crime of passion with no discipline, no strategy or forethought. It felt like a fairly logical escalation of Will's past behavior. *Damn it.*

"Ned Appleby's here," one of the deputies hissed from somewhere close behind Jericho. "Do you want him with you?"

"Yeah," Jericho said, keeping his voice low and calm. "Let's give that a try. Tell him to come up beside me but not go any farther."

Jericho stayed crouched down, just like Will, with his gaze somewhere over Will's shoulder. Nonthreatening, but paying enough attention that he'd be able to react quickly if Will started to move.

There was rustling in the duff behind him, then Mr. Appleby's voice. "Will, it's me. We need to get you out of here and clean you up, okay?" A pause, then, "This is Jericho Crewe. Do you remember him? He's going to take care of you. He's going to figure out what's going on, and he'll help us make things right again."

It was a pretty generous interpretation of Jericho's plans, but he didn't object.

"You need to come out of there, now," Mr. Appleby said. Will appeared to be listening, at least. His gaze was locked on the older man, and his body seemed coiled just a little less tightly. "You'd like to get cleaned up, wouldn't you? Like to have a good shave and go back to being your handsome self?"

Mr. Appleby started to ease his way closer, but stopped when Jericho put his arm out. "He could be armed," Jericho said.

"He'd never hurt me!"

"That may be what Lorraine Mackey believed," Jericho said. "I'm sorry, but if you can't get him to come out from a distance, we'll have to go in. Us, not you."

"He's scared, Jericho."

"That's when people are the most dangerous. No closer, Mr. Appleby."

Mr. Appleby clearly wasn't pleased, but then Will moved, just shifting his weight, and everyone refocused on him.

"Come on out of there," Mr. Appleby said again. "My Mary's worried about you. You don't want to worry her, do you?"

It was slow and painful, but Will gradually shuffled closer and closer to them. Jericho snuck his cuffs out as quietly and unobtrusively as he could manage and kept his eyes on Will's hands. No sign of a weapon, but his knuckles were bruised and scabbed over. Damn it, had he killed Lorraine with his bare hands? He was probably big enough—almost as tall as Jericho, and as wide, although with more fat, less muscle. He'd played baseball in high school, and football too, Jericho recalled with a pang. Back when he'd been himself, instead of the man the accident had made him into.

"Do you need to cuff him?" Mr. Appleby whispered. "He's calm now. He'll come without a fight."

"Cuffs are standard procedure." It was a bit of a cop-out, because he was happy to bend the rules when they seemed to be getting in the way, but this time, they made perfect sense. Will didn't need to get into any more trouble, and resisting arrest or assaulting a police officer would both make him look guiltier.

Another few minutes and Will was right out in front of them. Jericho nodded to one of the deputies to come close enough to assist, and then, as gently as he could, he eased Will's hands behind his back and slipped the cuffs on. Will made a horrible sobbing noise when the metal clicked shut, but otherwise remained impassive as Jericho frisked him and read him his rights.

"I'll drive him in," Jericho told the deputy. But really he was telling Mr. Appleby, telling him he'd do what he could to make sure Will was treated fairly. Respectfully, the way Mr. Appleby had always treated Jericho, even when he hadn't deserved it.

A crowd had gathered in the alley. There were the girls, their father, and several people who were probably neighbors; there was a middle-aged man who covered stories for the local paper; and, somehow inexplicably and yet inevitably, there was Wade Granger. He stood silently, a step or two away from the rest of the onlookers, and stared as Jericho led Will past the crowd.

There was a moment when it seemed like Will wasn't going to cooperate: he jerked away and tensed his whole body, ready to flee or fight. Jericho kept himself relaxed and just stood there for a while, eyes on the trees in someone's backyard, like a bird-watcher hoping to see a rare species. When he felt Will's shoulders slump, he quietly said, "It's not far to the station," and guided Will toward the cruiser.

That was when the man with the daughters spoke loudly into the silence. "See, girls? He's nothing! He's a pathetic retard, nothing to be scared of."

It took a split second for Will's gaze to find the man, and then he lunged toward him with a savage growl. Jericho had been so intent on keeping the tension from his body that he barely reacted in time. But he managed to hang on, and then the deputies were there, getting between Will and the crowd, pushing, wrestling, and finally shoving Will into the car, where he flopped on his side and cried in silent gasps.

Goddamn it. Jericho forced himself to remember Lorraine's battered face and lifeless body. She was the victim here, not Will Archer, and the deputies had responded with appropriate force to a threat against the public. Everything had gone the way it was supposed to go.

Still, as he headed for the driver's seat, he couldn't bring himself to look in Mr. Appleby's direction. He paused as he passed the man with the two daughters, and said, "We have your address? I'll be over tonight to take your statement."

"We already spoke to one of the deputies."

"Okay, I'll read that statement, and I'll come over to ask you some questions about it."

For a moment, the man didn't have his expression under control, and Jericho saw what he'd known was there. The petulance, the resentment, the desire to make life unpleasant for others. Jericho didn't think he was going to learn too much about the case at hand from this character, but he had other law enforcement responsibilities. A good cop knew the criminals in his neighborhood, but he also knew the assholes, the ones who followed the rules but still caused problems for everyone. This guy was pretty clearly an asshole, and Jericho wasn't going to pass up a chance to get to know him a little and figure out what he could about the guy's trouble-making tendencies. Besides, it would be nice to have a concern other than Will to think about at least temporarily.

The man's face immediately fell back into blank, slightly confused, but ultimately cooperative citizen mode. The mask he wore to make his dickishness socially acceptable. "Of course," he said. "We'll be in all evening."

"Thanks for your cooperation." Jericho slid into the cruiser and glanced through the plexiglass to see Will, still flopped over, lost in his private world of misery.

Jericho put the car in gear and eased it around the crowd and out toward the street. He still couldn't bring himself to look at Mr. Appleby. And, strangely, it was almost as hard to look in Wade's direction.

That was simply good thinking, he told himself as he headed toward the station. There was no reason to think about Wade, no reason to make contact with him, not in this situation or any other. Maybe Jericho was finally getting some common sense and giving a bit of attention to self-preservation.

That was what he wanted to be true, and he managed to believe it all through that evening. He got Will processed and settled in a holding cell at the station, contacted the public defender and arranged psychiatric consults for as soon as possible, did the paperwork, got the search warrant so he could send deputies over to Will's place to root around, and then he went to talk to Keith Wooderson, the asshole with the daughters.

The guy behaved exactly as Jericho had thought he would—he knew his rights and was damn well going to ensure that every one of them was respected. He gave Jericho the basic information about himself: he was forty-two, he worked as a web designer, he had no criminal record. He let Jericho speak to his daughters, but only with himself in the room. In most cases Jericho would have considered that good parenting, but in this case it felt controlling. It was enough to tweak Jericho's instincts to look for signs of child abuse, but nothing jumped out at him. Sometimes assholes were just assholes. So Jericho did his job, then went home exhausted.

But as soon as he pulled up in front of his building and saw the shadows by the front door move a little, he wasn't tired anymore. And as Wade separated himself from the darkness and stood in the semicircle of light from the building, Jericho realized that his common sense and self-preservation were still woefully underdeveloped. Talking to Wade was stupid, and he was absolutely going to do it anyway.

CHAPTER 5

Jericho didn't say anything as he unlocked the building's security door, just held it open and let that be his invitation for Wade to enter. They were silent as they shuffled up the stairs too, and even once they were inside Jericho's apartment, they were quiet until Jericho had led the way to the little kitchen, opened the fridge, twisted the lids off two beers and handed one to Wade.

Jericho remembered the last time they'd been together in the apartment: Wade had pulled a gun on him, and then—well, then things had gotten significantly more interesting. But that all felt like a dream, somehow. There was nothing contiguous about his relationship with Wade, only isolated, confusing scenes. Jericho tipped some beer into his mouth, then decided it was time to start the current episode of the Wade Show. "Why were you in the alley today? Please tell me you're not involved in this."

Wade blinked. Surprised. An apparently genuine reaction, followed by a smooth, fake Wade smile that seemed to waver at the edges. Damn it, had Jericho just hurt his feelings? "Lorraine Mackey was a friend of my mother's," Wade said. "I just—I don't know. I wanted to see it was being properly taken care of."

"As a concerned citizen."

"I guess so." He took a swallow of his beer, then looked at Jericho with eyes that were too bright and saw too damn much. "You're satisfied with how it's going? You're sure you've got the right guy?"

Jericho could physically hear the warning voice in his head. *You can't discuss an ongoing investigation with a known criminal, you idiot!* The voice was right, obviously, but Jericho's real voice said, "You give me your word, Wade? You tell me that this isn't one of your games, it isn't part of some new scheme to run drugs across the border using ex-athletes with brain injuries, it's just—just you and me, having a conversation about my day?"

Wade was still for a moment, then nodded. "I give you my word."

The word of a criminal, the word of the man who was the prime suspect in the death of Jericho's own father—it was completely meaningless. Except it wasn't, not with Wade standing there, staring Jericho right in the eye, unflinching.

"I'm not sure of anything." Jericho leaned back against the counter, trying to collect his thoughts. "Will's the logical suspect. He's the *only* suspect, so far, unless we want to say frail old Mr. Appleby beat a woman to death and strangled her with his bare hands."

There was something brittle in Wade's voice when he said, "That's what happened to Lorraine?"

Shit. "Sorry, yeah. Maybe you didn't need to know the details."

"She used to babysit me," Wade said. "Back when she was a teenager and I was a little kid. She was pretty messed up, even then, but . . . she was nice to me. She was kind."

"I didn't know her until I got back to town, and I only saw her when she was drunk or stoned, causing trouble. But I never saw her hurt anyone but herself."

Wade nodded, then raised his bottle. "To Lorraine. She never hurt anyone but herself."

Jericho lifted his own beer and took a swallow. As epitaphs went, it wasn't a bad one. "The problem is, it really looks like it was Will. Shit, Wade. Do you remember him in high school? He was a good guy. Just living his life, doing his thing, and then some drunk-driving asshole plows into him and turns him into Lennie. You remember Lennie, from that book we had to read with Mrs. Perkins?"

"Yeah." Wade looked down at his bottle, clearly surprised that it had somehow emptied itself. Then he scanned the kitchen, and unerringly headed toward the cupboard by the fridge where Jericho kept a bottle of Jim Beam.

Jericho drained his own beer and pulled two glasses out of the cupboard, and for a moment they were cozily domestic, working together to prepare, if not a meal, at least another form of vital sustenance.

They were in harmony right until Jericho reached into the freezer and pulled out the ice cube tray. Wade raised an eyebrow in amused disgust, and Jericho shrugged. "I have to work tomorrow. Sipping around the ice slows me down, keeps me from drinking too much."

"You got old."

"We're the same age, asshole." He dropped a couple of cubes into his glass and held the tray out temptingly. "Can I interest you in a little something?"

"Don't put yourself down, Jay. It's not that little."

It wasn't awkward, and didn't even make Jericho think of sex, not more than the shimmering haze of excitement he always felt when he was around Wade. It was Wade being Wade. So Jericho put the ice cubes back in the freezer and toed his shoes off, loosened his brown tie, and undid the first couple buttons of his beige shirt, then headed for the couch. He stopped halfway to undo his utility belt and leave it on the dining room table.

Yeah, he'd just disarmed himself and left the gun in easy reach of the known criminal who'd quite possibly killed his father. And he wasn't worried about it in the least. Damn, he was stupid.

But Wade followed behind him quietly, ignoring the gun, and slumped onto the opposite end of the couch from Jericho without comment.

They drank in silence for a while before Wade said, "The world's broken. That's not news to you. Lorraine had a rough time, turned into a drunk and an addict and a whore, ended up welcoming men into her house where she wasn't protected. And you know who hit Will? It was Sonny Quatrocchi, coming home from a hunting weekend with his two boys in the car. Had a couple beers as they were packing up their camp, got tested after the accident and blew just over the limit, ended up going to jail for it. Got out pretty quick but can't get a job anymore, not with this economy *plus* a criminal record, so he sits around the house, drinking all the time. He ruined his own life just as sure as he ruined Will's. And now his boys are growing up with a pissed-off drunk for a dad, so who the hell knows how they're going to end up. Will got bashed in the head, turns into someone he never was before, keeps it under control for a long time, but then gets set off by something and kills Lorraine. Nobody's a bad guy, nobody's a good guy. It's all just broken. And you can't fix it, not with all the laws you could ever come up with."

"So what are we supposed to do? Give up? Stop caring, stop trying to make anything better?" It wasn't a rhetorical question; Jericho really wanted to hear Wade's answer.

But Wade's shrug was noncommittal. "Keep trying if it helps you sleep at night. But don't get too worked up when it doesn't do you any good, you know?" His smile was fond and gentle. "You were always too much of an optimist. I feel like I spent half my high school years trying to keep the world from disappointing you. You and your Laws of Jericho—even then, you wanted to impose order on chaos. And even then, I knew it couldn't be done. But I wanted to believe, all the same."

Jericho stared at him, and Wade stared right back. "Why did you send me over to that meth lab?" Jericho asked quietly. "What was that about?"

Wade was quiet for a moment, then smiled, the quicksilver grin that was his version of a wink. "I heard he kept snakes. Thought that might be useful for you."

"You're so full of shit," Jericho said. "What the hell am I doing, talking to you? What possible excuse do I have for letting you in here, giving you drinks—"

"You're lonely." Wade made it sound like a simple fact. "You haven't got any friends in town, other than Kayla, and it's kinda awkward talking to her about this stuff, when she's your boss." He took a sip of his drink, then added, "And it's got to be hard to keep track of what you're allowed to tell her, right? How much can you pass along to her without her passing it along to her dad?"

"Jesus Christ, Wade, I can't talk to you about that!" Wade shouldn't even know about it. How the hell *did* he know?

Wade laughed. "But you can talk to me about everything else. And that's more than you can say for Kayla."

"*Everything* else?" Jericho didn't really want to do it. Didn't want to hear the denial if it wasn't going to feel real, and worse, didn't want to hear the confirmation. But he asked anyway. "So you'll tell me about my father's death? You'll tell me what happened there, and how you were involved?"

Wade didn't look guilty, exactly, but he didn't seem happy about the topic shift, either. "You know when to trust me, don't you, Jay? You know when I'm playing, and when I'm being serious?"

He waited for an answer, and Jericho slowly nodded. He *did* know, not that the knowledge ever seemed to do him any damn good.

"So trust me on this," Wade said. "Let go of that business. It's just one of those ways the world is broken, and you digging into it isn't going to make the world any *less* broken. It's too late to do anything about it, and honestly, I'm not sure you would have done anything if you could have."

"That's pretty fucking cryptic."

"The *world* is cryptic." Wade was quiet for a moment, then grinned. "You know what I wanted to say? A couple minutes ago, when you asked me what we're supposed to do in the face of a world that we can't fix?"

"Were you going to suggest I try narcotics?"

"I wasn't, but you're right, they are an option. But the plan I was going to mention was more along the lines of seizing the day. Taking pleasure where you find it. You know why I didn't say any of that?"

"Because it sounds like a cheesy pickup line?"

"Exactly." Wade's smile was warm, and Jericho wanted to bask in it. He wanted to forget about his father, and Lorraine and Will and Mr. Appleby. He just wanted to—damn it, he wanted to take pleasure where he found it. And if that pleasure was found in the smile of a known drug trafficker and suspected murderer? It would be awkward, but apparently not impossible.

"You after my virtue, Wade?"

"We traded whatever virtue either of us had when we were fifteen years old. I'm after something else, now."

Jericho knew what he should do. What he *had* to do. He had to stand up, show Wade to the door, and go to bed. Alone. He'd get a good night's sleep, wake up, and go back to work like a responsible adult. That was the only thing that made sense.

So of course he stayed completely still on the couch, cock hardening, waiting to see what Wade was going to do next. But Wade sat and waited as well, and finally Jericho collected himself enough to say, "You're after something else. Like what?"

Wade leaned forward and set his empty glass on the coffee table. "I'm honestly not quite sure. But it starts with—"

And then he moved, so fast Jericho could fool himself into thinking there was nothing he could have done to stop it. Wade's body hovered over Jericho's, their lips connecting, Wade's hands curled around Jericho's body, manipulating, rearranging, molding him to whatever purpose he desired. It all felt inevitable, and perfect.

Jericho was pretty sure he had the ability to actually turn off his conscious mind, or else maybe Wade had that ability. One way or the other, he was operating on instinct, and he liked it. When Wade maneuvered them so they were lying on the couch, legs entwined, mouths and groins lined up perfectly, Jericho's brain should have reminded him that Wade was an unsuitable partner; instead, it let him bring his leg up to wrap around Wade's and draw him in tighter.

"God, I missed you," Wade whispered, and that was enough to distract Jericho, at least temporarily.

"You can't keep saying that. I've been back for a while."

"I missed you since the last time I touched you." A deep, wet kiss, and then Wade said, "I'm *always* going to miss you since the last time I touched you."

Shit. Jericho couldn't let himself hear that, couldn't start thinking about *always* or anything else that wasn't happening right at the moment. "Bedroom," he suggested.

And Wade, the bastard, pulled away. "You sure? How's your boss going to feel about that? Your fed friend?"

"Are you planning to tell them about it?"

"No . . ."

"Neither am I." Jericho shifted, half rolled so he was free, and then stood up. "Come on."

Wade lay on the couch, staring up at him, his eyes impossibly gray, impossibly deep. "So I'm your dirty secret?"

"Jesus Christ, Wade, what are you looking for? You think we're going to date? You think I'm going to take you to the department picnic next month?"

"And that's more important? Saving face with your cop friends is more important than being true to yourself? To who you are?"

"What? Do you seriously think any of this is because I'm *gay*? Fuck that, anyone who doesn't know it isn't paying attention. But you're—" It didn't make sense that he was having to say this. Wade knew it already, knew it longer and better than Jericho did. "You're a criminal. You're the guy my 'cop friends' spend their days trying to arrest."

"*Some* of your 'cop friends,'" Wade said. He leaned back in his chair, his posture insolent and defiant. "But I've had cops on my payroll, and cops that come by my bar for drinks after work without worrying about my bad influence, or at least they did before the place burned down."

"Before you burned it down," Jericho corrected.

Wade didn't even acknowledge the interruption. "The only cops who have a problem with me are the fucking feds, and those bastards are so hung up on their fucking war against drugs that they don't care if they tear this town apart, don't care if they arrest every damn person living here, as long as they make sure the addicts in the cities keep paying top dollar for their smuggled-in shit."

"So the DEA is here with a price-fixing agenda? Is that what you're trying to tell me?"

"The DEA is just another player in the fucked-up game of the world." Wade leaned forward, his gaze intent. "No good guys, no bad guys. Remember? You think that only applies when brain-injured people kill whores? No, it *always* fucking applies."

"And that means I should just ignore everything? Ignore—" Damn, this wasn't going to sound good, and he knew it. "You break the law like it's nothing. You manipulate people—you manipulate *me*—like it's all a game. Shit, say it *is* all a game. Because games have sides, don't they? You and me, are we on the same side any way you try to set the game up?"

Wade seemed almost—no, not hurt, not for the second time in one day. Jericho couldn't accept that. But he seemed confused, surprised by Jericho's words. "You and me are always on the same side," he said as if it were an obvious truth, at least to him. "Any way that counts, any way that matters? We're on the same side."

Jericho stared at him. "So now maybe it's my turn to try to keep *you* from getting hurt by reality. I should try to keep the world from disappointing *you*. Because, fuck, Wade. We are *not* on the same side. Not according to the world. And not according to you a couple months ago. You remember that? You pulled a fucking gun on me, right over there?"

"I said 'any way that matters,'" Wade said gently. "I never mentioned anything about 'according to the world.' And it's not like I shot you."

"It's that easy for you? No, fuck that. If your criminal friends found out you were involved with me? Not using me, not buying information from me, but actually, sincerely *involved* with me? If your Canadian drug contacts knew you were dating an under-sheriff, if the Chicago connections you worked so hard to build found out, if the old crowd from your bar knew you cared about me—that would be totally fine with them? They'd celebrate your love, I'm fucking sure." Jericho was glad he was on his feet, because it was easier for him to step away from the couch, away from Wade. "Don't act like this is just me. It's not, and you know it."

"It's just you who's letting it get in the way."

"It's just me who has any damn sense, then."

Wade swung his legs around and surged to his feet, power and grace perfectly balanced even in such a simple movement. "Fine," he said. "You've got some damn sense. So why were you asking me to go to the bedroom?"

"Because fucking you isn't the problem here! God, if this was only about sex, everything would be easy. I've fucked lots of guys, and none of them caused me the trouble you do. None of them—" What? None of them mattered? That wasn't quite true, but it was true enough that Jericho didn't have the courage to say it out loud. "None of them had the history you and me have."

"There's nothing to be done about history."

"I don't even know what we're talking about anymore. I said bedroom, you said dirty secret, I said—what? What are we saying?"

"I think we're saying good night. I came over to check on you, that's all. I wanted to be sure you were okay. And you are, so mission accomplished."

"And am I going to find out that Nikki was off making some big border run or something tonight, and you just happen to have an iron-clad alibi by being here?"

"So suspicious, Jericho."

"I have every reason to be, and you damn well know it."

Wade's naughty-little-boy grin shouldn't have been charming. "I have no idea what you're talking about." He started for the door.

"Wait," Jericho said. Wade turned around. "Snakes. Did Cory Barker really have snakes in that house?"

"He did. You should ask the feds what they did with them; maybe Elijah can go visit them at animal control or something."

"He's not going to visit snakes anywhere they might be up for adoption. Nikki would kill me, and I couldn't blame her."

"They're a vilified animal, snakes are." Wade turned his back and took another step toward the door. "I've never had a problem with them. They just seem to be living according to their nature. You know?"

"You're not a snake, Wade. You're living the way you want, not the way you *have* to live."

"Well of course I'm not a snake. What a strange thing for you to say." And with that, Wade was out the door. He closed it gently behind him, and Jericho was left alone. Lonely, just as Wade had said.

CHAPTER 6

It was frustrating to talk to Will Archer. Probably frustrating for Will too, but he didn't show any signs of it. He didn't show signs of much, really. Jericho tried talking to him in his cell, got no response, and decided to take him up to the interview room to see if a change of scenery would do any good. Will didn't complain about being handcuffed, let himself be led, and then sat in the chair Jericho guided him to, his eyes locked on the mirror behind Jericho's back. The public defender sat beside Will and shook her head at Jericho.

"What do you actually hope to achieve, here?" she demanded. Typical young lawyer, aggressive for no reason. "He's mute. You're questioning an illiterate mute. You think he's going to confess via interpretive dance?"

"I'm not sure that would be admissible, but I'd love to see it, just for the artistic value."

"Even if he *could* speak, I'd be advising him not to. The prosecutor has already decided to lay charges, so what benefit could there be for my client to cooperate with you now?"

"He could exonerate himself." Jericho turned to Will. "If you could tell us what happened the night before last, we might be able to help you."

The lawyer leaned back in her chair, looking smug. "I've never had an easier client. I *know* this one isn't going to start blabbing and messing things up."

Jericho pulled out the sheet of paper and crayons he'd brought in with him. It was pretty damn close to interpretive dance and he wasn't sure if it would be admissible in court, but at least for investigative purposes it might be useful. "Could you draw me a picture, Will?

Could you show me what you were doing the other night? What happened at Lorraine Mackey's house?"

"My client will neither confirm nor deny that he was anywhere near that residence," the lawyer said, but Jericho ignored her.

Will was still staring over Jericho's shoulder. He'd shown no interest in the crayons or anything else since he sat down.

"You're really good at that," Jericho told him. "The no-eye-contact thing. I'm not bad at it myself—used to be military, went through all that 'don't you eyeball me' bullshit—but I'm a rookie compared to you. But it makes it kind of hard to have a conversation, you know? Any chance you could look at me? You don't have to talk, but you could nod or shake your head, if you wanted."

Apparently Will did *not* want, because he didn't shift his gaze.

Jericho had no strategies for this. He had a file of photos from the crime scene he could show a suspect, and he was pretty good at reading reactions, picking up on the tics people couldn't control. But he'd use those clues in order to form better questions and clearer accusations, ways to shake a prisoner's resolve and get him talking.

In this case? Will wasn't going to talk. There would be no confession. So questioning him seemed like a waste of time.

But surely it was wrong to not even try, to not give him *some* chance to defend himself against the charges.

Damn it. A noncommunicative suspect and a defense lawyer who was too green to look for compromises or take chances. Jericho was on his own with this one. He thanked the lawyer for her time and stood up. That was when Will reached for a crayon.

Jericho froze. The lawyer stretched for Will's hand, but the man jerked it away, holding on to the crayon tightly. "Don't take it from him," Jericho warned her, his voice as calm as he could make it. "You've given your warning; he's refused to listen. You've done your part, so now let him draw."

Will seemed oblivious to their conversation. He was hunched over the paper now, the crayon held awkwardly in his hands. Two circles, then lines, black wax bold against the white printer paper. It wasn't hard to figure out what Will was drawing.

A cartoon cat, the modified-snowman format that could be changed into a bunny with different ears and tail. A black-and-white cat. That was all. Maybe it was art therapy or something, but likely it was just a big waste of time.

Will stopped drawing, but stayed hunched over the page. Jericho and the lawyer waited, and after about thirty painful seconds, Will's right hand snuck out and put the black crayon back on the pile. For a moment, Jericho thought art time was over, but then Will's fingers poked through the crayons, and he lifted a new one delicately between his thumb and first finger. A red one.

Jericho and the lawyer both jumped when Will made a low growl and jerked the crayon toward his page. The strokes were wild, jagged spears of color, and Will emphasized each line with another low sound, almost a grunt. There was no pattern Jericho could see, just color, just an explosion of red covering the black-and-white picture.

The page was ripping and crumpling under the assault, and Jericho should probably take it away. The picture was evidence—evidence of something. But maybe it was also therapy, or release, or— He had no idea what the hell it was. But he left the page with Will until it was in jagged red shreds, and Will finally dropped the crayon. After a long moment of heavy breathing, he looked up, and his gaze returned to that imaginary spot over Jericho's shoulder.

"Shit," the lawyer whispered. "I'm not really trained for this."

"Me neither," Jericho admitted. "We've got a psychologist coming in to see him, but he should have another one from your side. And, I don't know, maybe he should have one for treatment or something? Someone to help him deal with . . . whatever."

"We've got a limited budget for an expert consultation. But we don't pay for therapy."

Of course they didn't. "Will you object if we try to figure an alternative out? Try to find a way for him to, I don't know, to get help?"

"The sheriff's department has a budget for that sort of thing?"

"No, not that I know of. But I can try to figure something out anyway."

She shrugged. "I'll have to consult, see about the pros and cons. Maybe an extra confidentiality clause? I'll look into it and get back to you."

They both stood up this time, but Will showed no sign that he noticed. Jericho spoke his name, then laid a hand on his shoulder to urge him to his feet, but Will shrugged him off angrily. Damn it, Jericho didn't want to have to wrestle this guy back down to his cell. "Hey, Will?" he tried. "We need to get some sweeping done downstairs. I heard you were good at sweeping, and it's an important job. Can you come help me sweep? That's what you do when there's no other jobs, right? It's time to sweep, Will."

And, miracle of miracles, Will rose to his feet and followed Jericho out of the room.

Manipulative. Using his disability and training in order to make your life more convenient. Treating him like a child. It was all probably true, but Jericho did it anyway. It was better than having to drag the guy down the stairs. *Sometimes the end justifies the means?* He felt positively Wade-like.

Shit, he shouldn't have thought of Wade. After getting Will back into his cell Jericho threw himself into his work, and when he went to Kayla's office later that morning to update her on the case, he didn't mention Wade's visit the night before. It wasn't relevant, and there was no need to bore her with details.

Instead, he reported the new information he'd found. "I contacted Will's social worker, a guardian assigned by the courts, but he kept Will on a pretty long leash. Said two violent incidents over seven years wasn't enough to upgrade the time allotted to his case."

"He's Will's legal guardian? I've been talking to the prosecutors' office about all this—it's possible Will could be declared incompetent to stand trial, but they want us to proceed with the investigation until someone makes us stop. They say the problem won't be his IQ or his ability to understand what's going on, it'll be his ability to communicate and help with his own defense. He could end up committed somewhere instead of convicted. But someone has to start that process. It doesn't sound like his social worker is going to be standing up for him?"

"Not soon, no."

"Anything else from him?"

"He said he doesn't know any specifics in this case, but it's not uncommon for people with brain injuries to use prostitutes. Their bodies still have the same urges, but their social skills may not allow them to meet people in the traditional ways. So—hookers, if they have the money."

"And Will had the money."

Jericho nodded. "He's not rich, but there was an insurance settlement, and Mr. Appleby was paying him. He didn't have a lot of expenses. So he could have afforded Lorraine's time, sure." It wasn't like she'd have been charging top dollar. "We didn't find any appointment book or even a list of clients when we were at Lorraine's house. No computer, no cell phone. But I checked the records from the last time she was arrested, and she had a phone on her then, so we're working with the phone companies to see if there's an account in her name."

"If there is, where's the phone?"

"Good question. She might have lost it, but if we find the account, we can check the usage records and see when she last had it."

"And we're getting nothing at all from Will?"

"I had a nice picture of a cat until he scribbled all over it. Kinda weird, but I can't think of a way to make it relevant to the investigation."

"Got the autopsy report yet?"

"Yeah." Jericho pointed to one of the files he'd brought in. "It says there *were* weapons used. Wood fragments in the contusions, and plastic fibers around her neck. They say not a baseball bat. The weapon was squared off, like a chunk of lumber. They think maybe a two-by-four. They're doing some more tests on the plastic, but they said it seemed like a feed bag, or something like it. That fake burlap stuff, you know? Called it 'woven polypropylene.'"

"She have any reason to have those items in the house?" Kayla's voice was quiet, but they both knew her question was vitally important.

"Maybe." Jericho had already thought it through, but it felt good to bounce ideas around with someone else. "Who doesn't have a couple chunks of lumber lying around? And a bag? Could have been grass seed."

"But those wouldn't be in the bedroom."

"Not likely," Jericho admitted. "So—shit, Kay, I don't know. If we're seeing it as a crime of passion, I could see Will doing it. But if we think there was premeditation? If the killer actually brought the tools in with him? Does Will still look like our guy?"

"He still looks like our number-one suspect. If you find someone better, fine, but until then? We dig for whatever evidence we can find." She seemed to sense Jericho's dissatisfaction with that answer. "I'll talk to the prosecuting attorney again. I want to push more on the competency issue—if his public defender is too weak to push for a hearing, maybe we should initiate one from our side so we don't end up going through an appeal. In the meantime, we need to find those weapons."

"I've got guys searching the woods behind the crime scene, all the way over to where we found Will yesterday. If we don't find anything in there, we'll widen the search area. But it's a big damn forest, Kay."

"I'll authorize overtime if we need it."

Jericho nodded. "Okay. I'm on it. Have we found a psychologist yet? Not necessarily for evidence"—it was hopelessly idealistic and naïve, but he said it anyway—"I want to find out what happened. It's not just about building a case. This isn't LA; these people aren't anonymous. I knew Lorraine, and I know Will, and . . . it's different up here. I don't want to win a case, I want to—to *know*. To do what's best for everyone."

"Welcome to small-town law enforcement." Kayla's tone was sardonic, but she softened it with a rueful smile. "I've made the request for a psych consult, but I'm not optimistic, not until there's a hearing to decide if Will can stand trial. So right now—investigate. By the book, so if we need it as evidence, we can use it. But even if Will doesn't go to trial, you're right—we still need to know what happened. Lorraine deserves that."

"We need to find the weapons," Jericho said, happy to get back on more solid investigative ground.

"Yeah."

"Okay." He pushed himself to his feet. "I'm on it."

"Hey, Jay?" Kayla said softly. She waited until she had his full attention, then said, "I just thought I'd mention—I was talking to Hockley this morning. He told me they've got surveillance on Wade Granger. He didn't say what for, but he said they're tracking his movements quite closely." A long pause and a piercing look before she added, "He thought you might want to know that."

Jericho's mouth was suddenly dry. "Oh," he croaked, and his brain stuttered, then kicked into gear. "Okay." How long had Wade been in his apartment the night before? Had they been near the windows at any point? And, shit, what did it mean that Hockley had told this to Kayla rather than going straight to Jericho with it? Was he expecting her to tell her dad, who would then tell Wade? Had Hockley just compromised a federal investigation in order to keep Jericho from getting caught in an embarrassing situation?

"I'm going to go help search for the murder weapons," he said, and practically ran down the stairs and out to his cruiser.

Goddamn it. He'd come out of the closet as soon as he'd left the military, and even when he was serving he'd relied on Don't Ask, Don't Tell rather than trying to be super-discrete. This fear of discovery, the awareness of how serious the repercussions could be if he got caught—he hadn't had to deal with any of that crap since the *last* time he'd lived in Mosely. He'd been sneaking around with Wade when they were kids too, but back then the forbidden aspect of it had been part of the fun. Now?

It wasn't fun. Now he had something to lose, and was old enough to know better, and didn't need the damn complication in his life. Hockley had given him a warning, and he needed to take it. Whatever he'd been playing at with Wade had to be over.

Maybe he needed to take a trip back to LA to get laid. He'd looked into the offerings in Montana, and it seemed like things were a lot more open than they'd been years ago, but he wasn't sure he was up to the headache of learning a whole new scene. Dancing made him feel like an idiot, and he didn't want to join a men's chorus or anything. He couldn't bring himself to accept the too-anonymous world of Grindr. Not when he could go back to LA, hit his favorite bar, and be naked and sweaty with a man of his choice within the hour. Meaningless and shallow? Hell yeah. Compared to the mess with Wade, meaningless and shallow sounded just about perfect.

So he'd work himself to exhaustion getting this case tidied up, and then he'd take a weekend off and get rid of some tension. He'd forget about Wade, and if the man made another visit, they'd have a brief conversation at the door, in full sight of whoever was tailing Wade, and then Jericho would go inside, alone.

It felt wrong, of course. His brain was telling him one thing, but his instincts, his loyalty, his damn emotions were all telling him something totally different. His body was definitely sending a clear message. But his brain had to win this time.

He drove slowly to the forest where the men were searching, but didn't want to disrupt their pattern by joining in. Instead, he ducked under the yellow police tape and made his way up the grassy gravel path that led from the alley to Lorraine's house. It was a little yard, poorly maintained, with five good-sized evergreens blocking views from either side. Probably deliberate, or at least an advantage, given the need for privacy in her line of work. A john could park down the street, duck in through the alley or even cut through the forest, and be in her backyard and then into her house without being seen. Jericho had checked the records and hadn't found a single arrest for anyone availing themselves of Lorraine's services, so there was no one to question about her business practices.

He peered around the yard. There was no bench, nowhere that looked like a waiting area. So she didn't seem to have been set up for drop-in clients, unless they'd dropped in so rarely there had been little chance of overlap. In LA, Jericho could have talked to someone in vice and gotten an idea of how things were usually done, but up here? Maybe Kayla would know. He'd ask her.

Someone called his name from the alley and he strode back in that direction.

"We've got something!" one of the deputies called to him, and Jericho jogged across the alley to the tree line. There was a smaller crowd today than the day before, but the reporter was there, standing near the deputy's cruiser, and a few people who were likely neighbors. Keith Wooderson, the asshole father, was one of them, and Jericho deliberately avoided eye contact with him. He didn't want to see the excitement on the man's face if they came out of the forest with the murder weapons.

"About a hundred yards back, buried under some branches and dirt," the deputy explained, hurrying along in front of Jericho. "We saw the disturbed soil first, and had to dig a little to be sure what we were finding. But once we saw a chunk of plastic, we left it."

"The lab guys are coming?"

"There was one of them working with us. He's taking pictures now."

By the time Jericho reached the site, the tech was carefully extracting the items from the ground, taking pictures at every stage. The rest of the crew stood and watched quietly. A strip of plastic about a yard long, maybe a chunk of cheap tarp or a feed bag. And a damn two-by-four, just as the lab had predicted, the pale-yellow wood stained with more than dirt.

"God, I can see the prints already," the tech muttered. He looked up and saw Jericho. "Really clear fingerprints, right in the blood. We'll get the results to you as soon as possible."

"By the end of the day?"

The tech nodded. "Sure, okay. I can take pictures here and see if they can match from that—honestly, I bet they can, they're so clear. But I'll have to drive it down to the lab for real confirmation. You won't get that until tomorrow."

"Give me what you can, as soon as you can."

The tech nodded, and Jericho turned to the rest of the team. "Continue the sweep, okay? You've started, you may as well keep searching. Anything unusual, anything that isn't part of a happy forest world, document it and let me know."

"There's a dead fox over by the ridge," Meeks, one of the newest deputies, said.

Well, that seemed unlikely to be important, but Jericho said, "Recently dead?"

"No. I'd guess a few weeks, maybe. Not much left but fur."

"I found a cat," Metsom contributed. He was another new deputy, obviously torn between excitement and disgust over his discovery. "Black and white. It was nailed to a tree."

Jericho turned to stare at him. "Nailed to a tree?"

Metsom nodded. "Kinda creepy." He shrugged, as if trying to seem blasé about it all. "But, you know—probably just kids. Not related to this, right?"

Except serial killers usually started with animal victims. And Will's picture had been a cat, before he'd slashed it all to hell with the red crayon. Shit. The MO was different—Lorraine hadn't been nailed to anything, hadn't been left in the woods. Still. "Take pictures, and then bag it up and send it to the crime lab. Tell them it came from near this crime scene, tell them to see if they can find a connection." He turned to Meeks. "You'd better do the same with the damn fox. And everybody else, add that to your list of things to look out for as you finish the sweep. We're looking for weird things, *especially* dead animals. Okay?"

The deputies agreed without discussion. They either knew why Jericho was concerned or they trusted him enough to act just because he'd asked them to. He tried not to wonder how that trust would be affected if they knew who he'd been drinking with the night before.

He should go to the station and brief Kayla on the new developments: the weapons he hoped would be useful, and the dead animals he hoped would be incidental. Instead, he wandered back into Lorraine's yard, and then into her house. The body had long been removed, of course, but the scene hadn't been cleaned up otherwise, and he could smell the heavy tang of blood that was starting to go bad. It was a too-familiar smell, and he thought again about his captain in LA. She thought he was heading for a burnout? Jesus, who *wouldn't* be? Who could immerse themselves in all this, the gore and the pain and the loss and the sheer futility of it, without it taking a toll? At least in LA there hadn't been the added intimacy of having known those involved; it would be ironic if the "vacation" in Mosely he'd joked about was actually what pushed him over the edge.

His years in the military had acquainted him with death, but it had been sudden, then: the bodies of his fallen comrades whisked away so quickly it was as if they'd never existed at all, and the bodies of his enemies even more remote. And he'd generally been able to fight back. If he'd done everything right, if he'd been tough enough and disciplined enough and paid close enough attention, he'd actually been able to protect people. He'd been able to prevent death, or at least prevent the death of the people on his side.

Working homicide? It was already too late by the time he'd been assigned to a case. Sure, there were some killers who needed to be stopped, men who needed to be taken off the streets before they killed again. But Jericho's job was to make the killers responsible for what they'd already done, not what they might do some day in the future. He wasn't helping anyone, because the person who needed help was already gone.

It was too late to help Lorraine. Maybe he'd had a chance, those times he'd dealt with her for being drunk or high in public, but he'd taken the easy way out. He'd written her a ticket, made sure she got home, and walked away. Shit, he'd *written her tickets*. He'd cost her money, money she'd had to earn by welcoming strange men into her home, into her body. He should have been part of the solution, and instead he'd been part of the problem.

He took a deep breath, trying to refocus, and picked up on something different in the air. Still not completely unfamiliar, and definitely nothing pleasant, but not gore, he didn't think. Another sniff, and he followed his nose to the closet by the back entrance. The closet door was ajar, and Jericho opened it carefully, peered inside, and found a litterbox, its surface covered in little twigs of desiccated cat shit. It looked like the litter had clumped itself solid beneath the shit, with so much soaked-up urine the cat hadn't been able to dig.

Jericho didn't know much about cats, but he was pretty sure he was inspecting the production of days or even weeks. This box wasn't a sign that there was a cat still living in the house for a day or two after its owner's death; it was a sign that Lorraine Mackey hadn't been good about cleaning her cat box.

Still, Jericho went to the kitchen and looked in the cupboards until he found a bag of cat treats, then pulled them out and shook them. It was his understanding that this sound was irresistible to any cats within hearing, but nothing in the house moved.

The cat wasn't there. Maybe it was outside, enjoying its freedom. Or maybe it was nailed to a tree in the goddamn forest.

CHAPTER 7

None of the neighbors seemed too impressed to have the law knocking on their doors for the second time in two days. They'd all made it clear the day before that they'd had minimal contact with Lorraine, but Jericho had hoped some of them would at least have noticed if she had a cat, and if so, what color it might be.

"We really don't have anything to do with people like her," he was told by a woman whose stark navy dress only partly covered her full sleeve of tattoos. "There are cats in the neighborhood, sure, but I have no idea who they belong to."

Nobody else knew, either. Jericho should go back to the station and work on getting Lorraine's phone records. If he had those, he could sort through the calls, looking for clients, or friends. But, he realized, he already knew one of her friends. Possibly her only one.

Sandi Granger was living in an apartment above a variety store on Main Street. The lock on the street-level door was broken, and Jericho pulled it open and headed up the stairs, expecting to find another door, the one to the actual apartment, at the top. Instead, he found himself standing in a living room, a woman glaring at him from the couch in front of the TV.

"Get the fuck out of here," Wade's mother growled at him, "or show me your warrant. You got a fucking warrant?"

Excellent start. "No, ma'am. I apologize for intruding—I didn't understand the layout of the place."

"The *layout*? You think having a floorplan would make it okay for you to invade my home without a warrant?"

In a way, it was nice to know that Jericho's general sense of befuddlement around Wade wasn't solely due to raging hormones.

It honestly seemed that there was something in the Granger nature that made Jericho feel like he was always being caught flat-footed. "I'm not here to cause any trouble," he tried, and held his hands out, palms up. "I don't know if you remember me, ma'am, but I'm Jericho Crewe. I went to school with Wade?"

"You did a hell of a lot more than go to school with him," she retorted. "But who you were then hasn't got a damn thing to do with who you are now. And just like I've told every other pig who wallows his way in here, I've got nothing to say."

"I'm not here about Wade, ma'am. Mostly not. But he did mention that you were a friend of Lorraine Mackey's, and I'm investigating her death. I was hoping I could ask you a few questions about her."

"I don't talk to cops," Sandi growled.

"I can understand that, but I'm truly hoping you'll make an exception in this case."

"Because you and Wade are so *close*?" Her sneer made Jericho think she knew exactly what had happened at his apartment the night before, but that was probably paranoia.

"No, ma'am. Nothing to do with Wade. I just thought you'd want to help me find the man who beat your friend with a two-by-four and then strangled her to death."

There was a short pause. "Is that supposed to shock me?"

"It shocked the hell out of me. I didn't know Lorraine that well, but seeing her like that, in her own damn house? It definitely made me want to catch whoever did it." He gathered his strength, then used his best bait. "I want that bad enough that I'm over here, humbling myself in front of someone who obviously has no use for me. I'm asking for your help, ma'am. I need it."

Apparently Sandi was either less perceptive or less bitter than her son, because she bit. "What do you need to know, exactly?"

"Let's start with the obvious. Do you have any idea who might have killed Lorraine?" Her sneer made her answer obvious, so he added, "Any difficult clients, anyone who had a grudge against her? A pimp or a dealer? Anyone?"

She squinted at him. "The Mountaineers used to send her some business, I think, before they all got busted. No one stepped in to pimp for her, not that I heard of."

"So no pimp. Maybe a dealer?"

"Mostly she drank, but the Mountaineers gave her some drugs too. But since they went away? I couldn't say where she was getting her stuff from."

Couldn't say because she didn't know, or because the new source was connected to Wade and she wouldn't turn in her son? Either way, pressing her wasn't going to make her change her mind, not unless Jericho was willing to get a hell of a lot more aggressive than he could justify. "What about clients? Anyone giving her a hard time?"

Sandi appeared thoughtful. Might just be an act, or might be he'd earned himself a bit of credit with her by not pushing too hard about the drugs. Finally she said, "Nobody lately. There was a guy a few months ago who got weird. She ended up spending a few nights down at the Lutheran church, hiding out from him."

The Lutheran church ran the only women's shelter in town, a couple of rooms in their basement that were available as needed. "Do you know the guy's name?"

Sandi shook her head. "No. She said he worked at the park. A ranger or something. But she hasn't mentioned him for a while."

"Anything else you can tell me about him?"

"She said he couldn't get it up. That's why he was such an asshole to her. Blamed her for it, said he wanted his money back, or else she had to give him a freebie some other time."

"I guess she probably didn't report any of that to the police, huh?"

"Probably not," Sandi agreed pointedly.

"Okay, well, anyone else you can think of?" Sandi shook her head, and he said, "Did she ever mention Will Archer to you?"

Sandi's chin jutted out as she said, "No." The no wasn't a denial so much as a refusal to answer.

Jericho likely wouldn't get her to budge on that, so he said, "Do you know how she kept track of her appointments? We're trying to figure out who she would have been booked to see that night, but we haven't found a calendar or anything."

"She had a little book. It should be there, in the house."

"Did you actually see it? Could you describe what it looked like?"

"It looked like a little book. You know, sheets of paper, connected together?"

"Color?"

"The paper was white. I don't know if it had a cover."

"You know where she kept it?"

"She kept it in the fucking house. Jesus, the place isn't that big. Just poke around."

Great. Another line of questioning that was taking him nowhere. "Do you know any of her other clients? Other than the guy from the park."

"A lady never tells."

"Meaning she didn't tell you, or *you* won't tell *me?*"

"Meaning fuck off."

Jericho had a sudden urge to introduce Sandi to Nikki. They'd probably get along. Or else kill each other. "It's likely that whoever killed her was one of her clients. So if you could give me any names, even just to rule people out—"

"Why are you asking me all that when you already caught the guy? That Will Archer, the retard from the hardware store."

"Person with a traumatic brain injury," Jericho corrected; it wasn't strategic to antagonize a witness, but damn it, Will deserved—Jericho had no idea what Will deserved. He needed to do his job, not get sidetracked. "Will Archer's a suspect, yes. That's why I was asking about him." Was it worth trying again? "Was he a client of hers?"

"I don't know." She frowned as if she'd surprised herself by answering this time, then shrugged. "Me and Lorraine weren't all that close, to be honest. Used to run together years ago, but since I got out of the business, we haven't spent as much time with each other."

"Okay. Are you aware of any other friends I could contact, or family?"

"No. She wasn't from around here. But I don't know where she was from. And no other friends. This town is—" She shook her head. "They're damn happy to decide what kind of person you are. And then they never change their minds. And she wasn't really looking for friends, anyway."

Jericho nodded. How much of the not-looking-for-friends was innate, how much was defensive, would probably never be known. "Uh, bit of a weird question, but did she have a cat that you know of?"

"Yeah. Tux. He's a nice little guy." For the first time, she seemed vaguely pleasant and interested in the conversation. "Who's taking care of him now?"

"Tux? Like Tuxedo. He's black and white, I imagine?"

"Yeah. You seen him?"

"Not in person." Jericho had no idea what it meant, if the cat in the woods was Lorraine's. Nothing good, although at least he wouldn't have to tell some neighborhood girl her pet had been murdered.

"I'll take him, if you can catch him. Maybe I should go over there and look for him. Is he outside?"

"Uh—we're not sure." No, that was too vague. He made himself say it. "It's possible he was killed, as well."

And there went the pleasantness. "'Possible'? What the hell does that mean?"

Was it reasonable to ask someone to make a victim identification for a cat? Probably not. "We've found a cat's body, but it wasn't in the house, and we're not sure it's his. Did he have any distinctive markings that you can think of, other than being black and white?"

"I don't know." Sandi seemed more shaken by the death of the cat than by that of her friend, but maybe that was because it was fresh news. "He— Lorraine always kept his claws trimmed way too short. I told her if she was going to let him go outside, he needed his claws to protect himself, but he dug his claws in when she petted him, so she trimmed them short."

"So the asshole who killed him didn't even get scratched."

She gave him a quick look, one that was a bit less hostile than the others. "Guess not. You're sure it was him, then? The cat you found?"

"Not sure, no. But I'll check the claws. Thanks." He decided to take advantage of her relative tractability and dug one of his cards out, then handed it to her. "You can reach me at those numbers, if you think of anything or hear anything. I'm not trying to cause trouble for anyone but the person who killed her."

"Yeah, that's real nice. But you don't need to *try* to cause trouble, do you? Eli Crewe's boy? Trouble's in your blood." She tilted her head, her expression caught halfway between crafty and demented. "You want my help with this? You have to do something for me."

He'd likely already gotten all the help she had to give, but he played along anyway. "What do you need?"

"You have to stay the fuck away from my boy. He's doing real well for himself, and he doesn't need you screwing things up."

Jericho wasn't sure what part of that to focus on: the idea that Wade's rapidly expanding criminal empire meant he was "doing well for himself"; the idea that *Jericho* was screwing things up for *Wade*; or the idea of expecting Jericho to stay away, when it was Wade who initiated almost all of their interactions. He settled on a noncommittal, "I'll keep that in mind. But I hope you'll get in touch regardless. I'm trying to find out who murdered your friend, so I assume we're on the same side for this."

"The same side?" She sneered at his uniform and snorted. "No, I don't think so."

It was such a complete reversal of Wade's perspective that it caught Jericho off guard. He'd argued with Wade, now he was disagreeing with Wade's mother, even though they were saying the opposite things. Damn, the Grangers were messing him up.

"I appreciate your time," he said. "Sorry for barging in. Please give me a call if you think of anything." And then he got the hell out of there before she made his confusion even worse.

CHAPTER 8

"Lay it out for me," Kayla ordered. She and Jericho were sitting in her office, both of them leaning back in their chairs and staring at the ceiling as if the answers to all their questions were written on the beige surface.

"We've got one suspect," Jericho said. "But if we don't get a match on the fingerprints, we don't have enough to hold him. That what the prosecutor said?"

"It is," Kayla agreed.

"I tracked down a guy from the national park who gave Lorraine a hard time a few months ago—he admitted it to me, seemed pretty freaked out by the whole situation. Solid alibi and doesn't give me a bad vibe. He's not our guy."

"So that's it? That's all we've got?"

Jericho sighed. "We've got a dead cat. Seems to be the victim's cat. I want a time of death for the critter, but from the pictures I saw, it's been dead for longer than Lorraine. I called down for them to check its nails, and were cut short, like Sandi said they would be. There are no 'missing cat' posters in the neighborhood or anything like that. It's almost certainly her cat." He paused to let her object to his conclusion, but she didn't. "So that's either a hell of a nasty coincidence or it suggests some level of stalking. The perp kills her cat, nails it to a tree. Kills her, with supplies that we think he brought with him. Takes her phone and her appointment book, which suggests that there was incriminating evidence in those items. So he was someone she knew, someone she had contact with. Someone who called her on the phone, or took calls from her, and I don't see our nonverbal suspect being the type to do either of those things, you know?"

"You believe he's innocent?"

"Honestly? Yeah. The psych report from the social worker says Will's operating at first to second percentile for most mental tasks. I guess he's better at some things than others, but overall, he's working at a pretty basic level. IQ, low seventies. I'm not saying our perp is a criminal mastermind, but he's thought parts of this through. And the only record of violence for Will has been spontaneous stuff, nothing premeditated. So this seems beyond his capabilities *and* out of character. The only evidence tying him to the crime is that he found the body."

"And was covered in blood," Kayla added. "The lab's analyzing his clothes now, trying to figure out a splatter pattern or anything else that would help us. It's difficult because he wore the clothes for quite a while before we got them, so there was a lot of smearing and contamination."

"He could have got bloody from trying to pick her up or something. He might not have known she was dead, might have tried to resuscitate her. There are definitely footprints in the blood at the scene, but they're too messed up to get a clear message out of them. So we hold him until we get the preliminary fingerprint analysis, and take it from there?"

"Sounds good," Kayla agreed.

"In the meantime, I'm going to kick up the gears on hunting for her phone records. I assume the phone itself has been destroyed, if the killer has any sense, and it'd be easy enough to burn an appointment book. There's no account under her name at any of the phone companies, so we're thinking she used prepaid cards. But if we can get the phone number, we can get the call records and see what the perp's trying to hide."

Jericho spent the rest of the day driving around to every place in town that might have ever gotten Lorraine's phone number from her. Doctor, dentist, bank, grocery store—they were all busts. Apparently she'd neglected her health and paid for her goods in cash, which made sense, given her source of income. The house was a rental; the landlord lived in town and went to visit her rather than calling. The man said he'd been happy to have the opportunity to check on his property and make sure it was still in reasonable shape, but Jericho got the feeling there was more to it. Like maybe the landlord had been willing to take out at least a little of his rent in trade. But there was no impression of violence from the guy, nothing that twigged Jericho's fairly well-developed instincts for sniffing out murderers.

His last stop came courtesy of Sandi Granger's information. The woman in the office at the Lutheran church had been a few years behind him in school, was welcoming enough, and seemed thrilled to be involved, even peripherally, in a criminal investigation.

"Technically, that's confidential information," she told him when he asked about the records they kept from their women's shelter, but she said it in a way that made it clear her objection wouldn't slow her down for long.

"It's really important that I know about this," Jericho tried, and gave her a mix of *sincere little boy* and *appreciative gentleman* in his smile.

She smiled back, said, "Hold tight," and wheeled her chair around to face a tall bookcase along the wall. She reached for a green binder, spun around and placed it on her desk, then flipped it open.

"You don't know the actual date she was here, do you?" she asked with a smile that was probably meant to be flirtatious.

Jericho smiled back. Never hurt to use what charm he had. "Uh, no, sorry. A few months ago, as I understand it."

"Hmm." She flipped a few pages. "I remember her being here. There was a woman with two kids in at the same time, and I was worried that the mom wouldn't like her kids hanging out with—well, you know—but the mom wasn't worried at all. And then I saw more of the mom and kids and started to wonder if maybe it should be Lorraine I was worrying about protecting."

It was just idle chatter. There were plenty of rough women with two kids in the Mosely area. Absolutely no reason for Jericho's radar to be pinging. But when the woman behind the desk triumphantly said, "There she is," Jericho let his curiosity get the better of him.

He craned his neck as if he was trying to see the listing, but really he was looking at the one directly above it. *Nikki C., with two children.* Reason shelter needed was marked with *not given*, of course, because Nikki wasn't the sort to share her troubles with a stranger.

Goddamn it.

Nikki had taken the kids to a women's shelter. Maybe he could twist it around, try to make it something more palatable, but he forced himself to see the truth.

Jericho had run away, and his dad had stayed behind and he hadn't changed. He'd been an abusive asshole with Jericho, and then he'd been an abusive asshole with someone else.

Had it been Nikki or the kids? All of them? Yeah, all of them, because if someone in the home was getting beat up, it hurt everyone living there even if only one person was getting hit.

He'd known what his father was, and he'd walked away. Never made a police report, never bothered to have the damn conversation, never told Eli that beating on people weaker than him was a coward's way out and he was no kind of man if he ever did it again. No, Jericho hadn't thought about anyone but himself; he hadn't done a thing to help Nikki and the kids.

He might not have been part of the problem, but he sure as hell hadn't been part of the solution. It wasn't just Lorraine he'd let down.

"I'll write that number down for you," the woman behind the desk said. She was frowning gently at him, like he'd been staring at the book for too long, and Jericho had to fight to remember what she was talking about.

"That'd be great," he managed. "Thanks."

She beamed at him. "I'm happy to help."

He took the slip of paper she offered him and stumbled out of the office, then down to the street where his cruiser was parked. When he reached the car he didn't get in, though. Instead, he carefully tucked the paper into his jacket pocket and leaned back against the hood. Things in Mosely never really changed; they just looped around back to the beginning and started the same patterns all over again.

CHAPTER 9

Jericho got back to the station to find the preliminary fingerprint report waiting for him. He opened the emailed file with trepidation. Were things about to get much simpler or much more complicated?

There were the standard words of warning about the preliminary nature of the results, but Jericho skimmed over those. He wasn't looking to introduce evidence into court, he just wanted to know if he had the right person sitting in a holding cell.

And apparently he did. He stared at the screen and realized he'd been expecting the report to come back with someone else's prints. He'd honestly thought Will was innocent, but the prints were crystal clear.

Still his brain raced, trying to explain things away. Maybe Will had picked up the weapons at the same time he discovered the body. That made sense. But then he'd taken them into the forest and buried them, which was a pretty obvious indicator of guilt.

Maybe he hadn't been the person who buried them? Will could have gone to the house, found the body, touched the weapons, splashed around in the damn blood like he was pretending to be a paint roller, then left, and someone else had come in, taken the weapons with Will's prints on them, and buried them. That . . . that was stretching it.

If you hear hoofbeats, think horses, not zebras, he reminded himself. The simplest explanation was almost always the right one. He needed to base his decisions on facts, not wishes. So he'd let the prosecutor know about the fingerprints, the prosecutor would lay charges, and Jericho would focus on finding more evidence for the trial. That was how the system worked.

He set one of the deputies to getting the phone records for the number he'd gotten at the church, changed into his workout clothes, and took an extra-long run on the way home. If he was tired enough, maybe he'd be able to stop thinking.

But as he ran, his brain kept working. What had Will been thinking? Feeling? Had he been afraid or angry?

He could practically hear Wade lecturing him. *There isn't just one reason for most things, Jay. The world is a complicated place, and people do things for complicated reasons.*

At least thinking of Wade let him obsess about something different for a while—like what the hell Sandi Granger had thought she was talking about, warning Jericho away from Wade for *Wade's* sake. Jericho needed to stay the hell away from Wade, sure, but that was to protect himself, not Wade. Wade was fine. He was fluid, completely malleable, able to adapt to any conditions he encountered. Wade was *always* fine. That was part of what made him Wade.

Unlike Will. Will, sitting in a jail cell, about to be charged with murder. Jericho wanted justice for Lorraine Mackey, and it was his damn job to find the killer. But putting Will away just didn't feel right.

Too many deaths, too few real solutions to anything. Wade had spoken the truth: the world really was broken.

Jericho finished his run, went home, and did sit-ups and push-ups in all variations until every muscle in his body was shaking, then took a glass of bourbon into the shower with him. After that, he managed to fall asleep.

He got to work early the next morning and went over the evidence against Will. When the telephone report came in on the number he'd gotten from the church, he wasn't surprised to find that the last call that had been answered by her phone had come from the hardware store, about a quarter of an hour before closing on the night she'd been killed.

"Okay," Kayla said with a sigh, after he shared the latest updates with her. "I'll pass it along to the prosecutor, but she was planning to charge Will already, with only the fingerprints. The phone call, and whatever else we come up with now—they're for the trial, assuming he's found competent. They're ways to prove what we already know."

"I don't think he did it," Jericho said.

Kayla stared at him. "What? I know you were unsure, Jay, but you just gave me another piece of totally damning evidence, and it's convinced you that he *didn't* do it?"

"It's too tidy. The world is messy, Kay. When do things fall together this smoothly in a real investigation?"

"It's not like he's a criminal mastermind. That's why it hasn't been that hard to catch him—don't look a gift horse in the mouth."

"No, it's *too* tidy. He called from the hardware store? He doesn't talk, Kay. Not really, not on demand. I'm not sure he can even dial a phone—I'll have to ask Mr. Appleby about that."

"The call came from the store—that's confirmed. So if it wasn't Will, who the hell was it? Are you suggesting Mr. Appleby was visiting prostitutes in his spare time?"

"The phone in that store is beside the cash register, and Mr. Appleby often works alone. If he was somewhere else in the store helping a customer, it'd be easy for someone to lean over and make a call. There aren't any security cameras that will help us with this, and the call only lasted fourteen seconds. Enough for an 'I'm coming over,' but not long enough for anyone to notice some stranger behind the counter."

"You're suggesting someone framed Will? Why would anyone do that?"

"To cover their own crime. He's an easy target, right? Can't speak up to defend himself, has a history of violence. We haven't found the appointment book, yet, but if we do, maybe we'll find Will's name in it; that'd be another piece of incriminating evidence, but still only circumstantial."

Kayla pinched the bridge of her nose and leaned back in her chair. "It is too early in the day for me to be this exhausted."

"I know it's a stretch, Kay, but the case honestly doesn't feel right."

"Because it's *too* right. That's what you're telling me. Your determination to make my life more complicated than it needs to be has actually extended to the point that when we're faced with a simple, straightforward answer, you reject it automatically. Is that an accurate summary of your position?"

"Do you really think he did it? I don't mean what your brain tells you, but your gut. Your instinct. When you look at Will Archer, do you see a killer?"

"Courts don't care about my *gut*, Jay! They care about evidence."

"We're not in court. We're here, in your office, you and me. Right here—do you truly think Will Archer killed Lorraine Mackey?"

"If I say yes, will you let this go? Will you go back to quietly gathering incriminating evidence, as directed by the prosecuting attorney?"

Jericho stared at her. "*Are* you saying yes? You've been a cop for longer than I have. Maybe fewer murders, but you know how to read people. You know Mosely. If you say you honestly think Will did this? I'll— I don't know. That would go a long way toward shutting me up, yeah."

She gave him a look, her face neutral before it changed to a grimace and let out a dramatic groan. "Keep digging. Be as discrete as you can, because the prosecutor is going to be pissed if she hears we're still hunting for other suspects after she's charged Will with the crime. But—" She stopped, obviously choosing her next words carefully. "I don't know if I truly believe he's innocent or I just *want* to believe he's innocent. But in either case, we need to be sure. Have you got someone in mind for the alternative suspect?"

Jericho grimaced. "Not really. I mean, not anyone I have any evidence on, whatsoever."

"But . . ." she prompted.

"There's something not right about Keith Wooderson, the guy who says Will was menacing his daughters? He claimed the girls had to watch Will come out from the forest for closure, but they barely seemed interested at all. But *he* was fascinated. Excited. And I checked the visitor book for Will. Both Applebys have been to see him, but other than that? One guy. Wooderson. And it's not like the bastard was acting out of compassion, not based on the way he was talking about Will. I know it's a long shot—he's almost certainly another suburban dad hungry for some action in his life, but I want to do a bit more digging. It's instinct, that's all."

Kayla didn't seem impressed, but that was okay. He wouldn't be impressed, either, if someone came to him with such a vague idea. He just needed to poke around a little. If he found something on Wooderson, that would be great. If he didn't, he'd keep poking. It was his job to find the *right* person to convict, not the easy one.

"Instinct." Kayla's gaze was assessing, and Jericho straightened, trying to look responsible and wise instead of lost and confused. "Tempered with experience. That's why I tagged you to head up the investigation. So I'd better not second-guess myself now. It's still your show, Jay. Don't let me down. Don't let Lorraine down."

He nodded and left her office. He wouldn't let them down and wouldn't let *Will* down either. He wouldn't let the citizens of Mosely down. If Will killed Lorraine, he needed to be dealt with; but if he didn't kill her, that meant somebody else did. Somebody currently walking around free, able to kill again.

CHAPTER 10

"I know it takes time to do a full report, and I truly appreciate you getting the preliminary one to us early. Seriously, that was great. But what I'm asking now is—could the prints have been faked? Is there any way for you to *test* if they were faked?"

Jericho already knew the answer to both questions; he wasn't a total rookie. But he didn't want to come across like some big-city big shot trying to teach the locals how to do their job. So he waited quietly, and finally the fingerprint tech said, "Yes. It *is* possible to fake fingerprints. That's usually something we expect to see in technological applications, though—identity theft or that sort of thing."

"Yeah, I know it's a long shot, but I'd like your expert opinion on it all the same. Like, is there *anything* weird about the prints? Or, I don't know, could you do a test, see if there were any traces of synthetics on the source material, or—you know what to look for, obviously. But if there was anything like that, it would be great to hear about it."

"It would be?" The tech sounded genuinely confused. "Usually the police aren't hoping for ways to weaken their own evidence."

"Well, I didn't mean 'great' like that's what I want. I just meant it would be better to hear about it now than at trial, you know?"

"Yeah, okay," the tech said cautiously. "I'll see what I can find. Okay?"

"I'd appreciate it. Thanks."

Jericho set the phone down. One job down, but quite a few more to go.

The next task took him out of the office. He hadn't been inside the elementary school since his own days attending; on a couple of occasions he'd been called to deal with Elijah's nonsense, but he'd always managed to sort things out off-property or in the parking lot. Now, though, he was going in. It was still a week or so until school started, but there were cars on the gravel in front of the building; some of the staff, at least, were at work.

He took a deep breath, pulled open the front doors, and headed for the office. When he arrived, the woman behind the desk was far too familiar. "Mrs. Andarov?"

She looked up, squinted, and then accused, "Jericho Crewe."

Damn, the woman had seemed old when Jericho had been a student, but maybe that had just been a child's perception. Now, though, twenty years later, she was absolutely ancient. Why did she still have a job? *How* did she still have a job? And how the hell had she recognized him?

"Mrs. Andarov. Wow. It's good to see you."

"Because you have such fond memories of your visits to the office?" she asked dryly. Her accent remained strong, and he idly remembered the gossip about her being a Soviet spy. "I heard you were back in town. I was a little surprised to hear your profession, I admit."

"Yeah, you're not the only one. I guess back in those days I was just searching for some structure, you know? I needed discipline to give me a sense of my place in the universe."

"Don't get sassy with me, Jericho."

"Sorry." He hadn't thought she'd catch the sarcasm.

"Are you here about Elijah or about Nicolette?"

"Uh, neither, actually. Unless I need to be? Are they okay?"

She raised an eyebrow, making it obvious that *okay* was a relative term. "School is out, so I am unaware of any crises. But if you're not here for them—"

"Wait. You're right, I'm not here for them. But, off the record—" He tried his best panty-dropping smile and was rewarded with an impatient grimace. "Uh, off the record, *are* they okay? And even further off the record—was there a time when they weren't?"

"I think you need to be more precise in your questioning."

Jesus. She might be old, but she sure hadn't softened over the years. "I don't mean to be blunt, but have you had any reason to expect that they were being . . . abused? That things were difficult at home?"

"They were living with your father. Is that not enough reason for us to suspect abuse?"

Jericho wasn't sure he'd ever been made to feel so personally guilty for his father's failings. It was as if Mrs. Andarov had tapped right into his self-recriminations and decided they were completely accurate. "Other than that? Did you ever see anything concrete?"

She frowned. "Why are you asking?"

"I just want to know what I'm dealing with. I'm trying to take a more active role in their lives, but that would be easier if I knew what they were up against. What their past was like."

"You should pay less attention to their past, and convince them to concentrate on their future."

Jericho didn't have the patience for this, but he forced himself to smile. "That's great advice. Thank you." And maybe it was time to move on. "Actually, I'm here for a different reason. I'm looking for a previous address for a couple of your students—Miranda and Alisha Wooderson. They would have transferred in sometime in the fall, as I understand it. Can you tell me where they came from?" Because Keith Wooderson had said it was none of Jericho's business, and there was something about that refusal that had made Jericho's instincts kick in. Maybe he was just being a bully, trying to enforce authority he didn't have. Or maybe there was a dodgy vibe about Wooderson. Damn, he needed to be careful, because he was really *hoping* there was something dodgy about Wooderson, and that sort of predisposition wasn't going to produce good police work.

Luckily, Mrs. Andarov seemed unconcerned with Jericho's inner turmoil and willing to cooperate. "Such nice girls," she said as she stood up and headed for a long filing cabinet along the back of the room. "A little quiet, but that's a nice change from all the rowdiness."

She cast an accusing look over her shoulder, clearly thinking Jericho was responsible for at least some of the noise that came through her office. Was she still flashing back to his own days in the school, or did she think he had the power to control Elijah and Nicolette and was just refusing to use it?

"Oh, here we go," she finally said. "They came to us from Akron, Ohio. Jefferson Lake Elementary."

"And do you know anything about their mother? Is she living with them?"

Mrs. Andarov shook her head. "Oh, no. We have instructions not to let her anywhere near the children. Mr. Wooderson has full custody. If she shows up, we're supposed to call—well, we're supposed to call you or your colleagues."

"But she hasn't been seen since they've been here?"

"No," Mrs. Andarov said. She sounded a little sad, as if she'd have welcomed the excitement of an in-office battle.

"You have the custody papers, though? Copies of them? Would you be able to give me the address she was using when they were written?"

"What's all this about, Jericho? Is there a problem with Mr. Wooderson?"

"No, not really. Just doing a bit of background checking. You know how it is—better to be prepared."

She didn't seem completely convinced, but she copied the information down anyway and passed the sheet of paper across her desk. Anne Wooderson had been living in Akron when she'd lost custody of her daughters. Hopefully she was still there, or somewhere near enough that Jericho could find her. He had a feeling she might have some interesting things to say about her ex-husband.

CHAPTER 11

Jericho could tell something was up as soon as he stepped inside the sheriff's building. Deputy Garron was at the front desk, as usual, and there was nothing *obviously* wrong. But there were too many people in the front area, and they all seemed to be standing around, not doing anything.

Jericho gave Garron a questioning look, and Garron raised an eyebrow in return. "There's someone here to talk to you about the Mackey case," he said.

Jericho turned toward the plastic bench and plastic plants that made up the station's waiting area, and saw Wade Granger rise gracefully to greet him. "Under-sheriff," Wade said calmly, with no acknowledgment of the waiting crowd. No smirk to show he knew what a scene he was making, no frown at the thought of the many, many times he'd been taken through this space in handcuffs. "I came across some information I thought you might find helpful in regards to Lorraine Mackey. Is this a good time to share it?"

"Sure," Jericho said, trying to match Wade's casual tone and failing entirely. "Come on upstairs."

"I'd prefer to avoid the interrogation rooms, if you don't mind," Wade said as he fell in beside Jericho. "I think I've spent enough time in those."

"My office okay?"

"Sounds lovely," Wade said.

"You don't mind if we ask Kay to sit in? She's working the case with me." And it would seem a lot more professional if Jericho had a witness to the conversation.

For the first time, there was the tiniest hesitation from Wade, just the slightest hint that things weren't going absolutely, positively according to his plan. But of course he recovered quickly. "Always lovely to visit with an old friend."

Kayla's door was open when Jericho reached it, and when he leaned in and said, "Can I borrow you for a couple minutes?" she stood up without asking why. Probably because she damn well knew why, but had been respectful enough to not join the crowd watching the spectacle downstairs.

"Kay, good to see you," Wade said with exaggerated courtesy as she joined them. "You're looking as lovely as always."

"Don't push it, Wade," she warned, and he grinned.

Jericho got them into his office, shut the door, and then sat in his chair behind the desk, pulling a pad of paper over in front of him, ready to take notes. This was business. Just because he could smell Wade's cologne, just because he knew what Wade's skin tasted like and how the man would react if Jericho dragged his teeth across that patch of skin showing at the neck of his shirt—none of that mattered. Wade was here on business. "You have something to tell us about the Mackey case?" he asked, his voice only a little tighter than usual.

"No time for small talk with an old friend and, now, valued source of information?"

"Hey, Wade, how've you been?" *Did Kay's dad tell you the feds have a tail on you? Is that why you're here instead of coming to my apartment? Or have you known about the tail all along, and just didn't bother to tell me?* "I saw your mother the other day. She's looking well."

"Funny you should mention her. She's actually why I'm here."

"Is that right?"

"It is." Wade leaned back in his chair, giving the impression of a pompous professor about to deliver a lecture to an ignorant but knowledge-hungry undergrad. There was absolutely no reason for it to be turning Jericho on. No reason other than Wade. "She told me about the questions you asked her, and I sensed that she might not have been quite as forthcoming as you could have wished."

"If you mean she told me to 'fuck off,' then—"

"Now, Jay. She told me she gave you some good information. She said she told you almost everything she knew about the situation."

"*Almost* everything?" Kayla asked.

Wade raised his eyebrows at her, clearly expressing his displeasure at her interjection into a conversation that had been going so smoothly without her. "Wade," Jericho said. "Seriously, don't push it. What extra information did your mother have?"

And that was another thing that shouldn't have been sexy: Wade's mock prissy face. The pinched-in mouth, the eyes opened overly wide—they should have made Jericho think of someone's annoying great-aunt. But, somehow, on Wade, the effect was— Oh, it was hopeless. There was nothing Wade could do that would make Jericho not want him.

So maybe Jericho was a bit more aggressive than the situation warranted when he said, "Fuck you, Wade, I'm not going to beg you. You came all the way here to tell me something, so tell me without the games. Okay?"

Wade turned to Kayla. "Do you allow your staff to swear at members of the public?"

"In some cases I encourage it."

"Wade," Jericho said. It was strangely gratifying to see Wade's grimace as he turned his head toward Jericho as if compelled by the same absurd attraction that made Wade's own requests so hard for Jericho to ignore. And as if Wade found that compulsion just as frustrating as Jericho did. "What did your mother tell you?" Jericho asked, and he kept his voice gentle out of compassion for himself, as much as Wade. They were both stuck in this obsession together, so they might as well try to be pleasant.

"She told me Will Archer *was* one of Lorraine's johns," Wade said reluctantly. "She said Lorraine told her he was sweet. Got too excited sometimes, but overall sweet. He'd bring her presents, apparently. Flowers—like, handpicked, not bought—and weird things like a kid would give you. A shiny rock, or a feather, or something. My mom said the cat was dead? Somebody killed it?"

"Not completely positive, but, yeah, it seems likely."

"My mom said Lorraine told her Will loved that cat. Brought it treats every time he visited, played with it, snuggled it—whatever. He was at the house for pussy, in every possible way."

"That's lovely, Wade," Kay said.

But, strangely, it was. Well, not Wade's crude "pussy" comments. But Kay's response, Wade's grin back at her, and Jericho, part of it all, watching two of his favorite people scrap and squabble as if they were comfortable with each other, comfortable even if they didn't get along. It felt like family, or at least like family was *supposed* to feel.

But then he dragged himself back to reality. Will had been gentle with the cat and brought it presents, and the cat had ended up dead. Will had been gentle with Lorraine and brought her presents, and she'd ended up dead. He couldn't forget Will's crayon drawing, the simple animal, and then the violent, red destruction.

"He knew the cat was dead," he said out loud. "He either killed it himself, saw it being killed, or saw it soon after, when it was still dripping blood. And obviously the same with Lorraine; he was covered in her blood like it had been fresh when he found her."

"*Found* her?" Wade asked carefully. "You're saying he didn't kill her?"

"No, he's not saying that," Kayla said quickly. "Right, Jericho?"

"I'm not saying that," he repeated obediently. Then he looked at her and said, "But if my theory's right—if he was framed—then he might know who *did* kill them. Either the cat or Lorraine, or maybe both of them. If he was there that soon after they died, he might easily have seen the actual killing. He could know who did it, and we have no way to get that information out of him."

"Show him pictures," Wade suggested. "Have you guys got alternate suspects? Do a lineup, or something. Let him go right in the room with them and point out the guy who did it."

"Shit, maybe he already did," Jericho said, thinking as he spoke. "When we went to pick him up in the forest—" The realization blazed in his mind. "Wooderson was there, being a smug son of a bitch, and Will lunged at him. I thought it was because Wooderson had said something insulting, but would Will even have understood that? Or was he just reacting to the bastard's face?"

"I'll have to talk to the prosecutor," Kayla said reluctantly. "She just about had a coronary when I told her we were investigating different suspects. She's not going to be a hell of a lot happier when I start asking her about the admissibility of nonverbal evidence."

"But you'll do it," Jericho said. Kay would do her job, because she was Kay. And speaking of people following their natures— "Wade, have you got an angle on this? I need you to look me in the eye and tell me straight. Do you have some sort of a plan, here? Some way to get what you want out of this, some manipulation of the system—some manipulation of *me*—to turn it to your advantage?"

Wade was quiet for a moment. "This isn't the first time you've asked me something like that; I suppose I should be hurt by your suspicion." Then he turned his face up, his gray eyes intense and true as he stared at Jericho. "But I'm not. I've earned it, and I'll probably earn it again. But right now, Jay? For this situation only? My mother was a friend of Lorraine's, and I never had a problem with Will Archer, which is more than I can say for most of the idiots we went to school with. I came here for my mother, because she wanted me to pass information along. But if that information is being used to help Will get out of this mess? That would make me very happy, Jay, and that's my only ulterior motive."

Jericho wanted to simply accept that, but he tried to make his brain sort through it all, searching for the twist, the trap. "Could you simplify it a bit, for me? Could you just tell me, yes or no: are you telling me the truth, the whole truth, and nothing but the truth on this one?"

"I do solemnly swear," Wade intoned. "I'm afraid a Bible might catch fire if I laid hands on it, but I'll swear on—" He peered around the room for a moment before his gaze cut back to Jericho. "I'll swear it on *you*, Jay. I'm not playing any games with this one."

"Okay," Jericho said past the knot in his throat. This perfect, beautiful, maddening man, out of reach even though he sat right across the desk. "Thank you."

Wade smiled at him, and for a moment Kayla wasn't there, the sheriff's department wasn't there, not a single human being in Mosely was there. It was just Wade and Jericho, away on some mountain somewhere, together. Then Kayla shifted, Jericho blinked, and he was back at work, two old friends across the desk from him.

"You're still looking for a list of Lorraine's johns?" Wade asked.

Jericho nodded and tried to refocus. "We haven't found the phone or the appointment book yet. So, yeah, other than Will, we don't know who she was working for."

"My mother says she doesn't know, but I can ask around. I won't get everybody, but there are people who will talk to me who would never talk to you, right?"

"It's not a good idea for you to insinuate yourself into this investigation," Kayla said.

Jericho frowned at her. "Come on, Kay. We use CIs all the time. How is this different?"

"I think we all know exactly how it's different. Jay, it's not good for you to be too . . . involved with Wade. You know that."

Wade said, "I'm not sure about that. But I've got to say, I'm a bit insulted by the CI bit. That stands for '*criminal* informant,' doesn't it? Seems a bit slanderous toward someone who's never been convicted."

Jericho snorted in disbelief. "Bullshit you've never been convicted! We both were. Possession, assault, trespass—they weren't felonies, but they were crimes."

"So you're a fellow criminal?" Wade's voice was silky smooth, inviting confidences, admissions, and intimacy.

"This is completely off topic," Kayla interjected. "The point is— Damn it, you both know what the point is. This isn't about Wade, it's about the two of you, together. *That's* what makes it not a good idea."

"I'm suggesting we exchange information, not bodily fluids," Wade replied. "Nothing to be alarmed about."

"The fact that you've already morphed this into 'exchanging' information is absolutely something to be alarmed about." She frowned at Jericho, then turned back to Wade. "You can go through me," she said. "Any information you get, we'd truly appreciate. You can give me a call or come by whenever it's convenient."

Wade's eyes narrowed, making them a darker, more dangerous shade of gray. "You protecting your boy's virtue from the Big Bad Wade? You think that's necessary?"

"I'm protecting my employee's career from an unnecessarily awkward situation." She paused, then nodded decisively. "Jay, anything having to do with Wade and police business will go through me. If you choose to see him on your own time?" She shook her head. "You know how I feel about that, and you know how it could affect your career. So do what you want, but don't pretend you're doing it for the department. Don't pretend it to yourself, and don't you dare pretend it to me." She turned back to Wade and her voice was firm. "If it's police business, you can give me a call, not Jericho."

"*I* don't work for you, Sheriff," Wade said. "You can order Jay around, apparently, but not me. If I, out of the goodness of my heart, decide to use my local contacts to find some useful information for your investigation, I'll give it to the department through whichever officer I choose."

Kayla shook her head at Jericho. "If there actually *was* any goodness in his heart, he'd give us the information without a bunch of conditions. And if he actually cared about you rather than about himself, about his ego and the thrill he gets from showing up the sheriff's department, then he'd stay away from you and let you get on with your life."

Jericho felt like the angel and the devil on his shoulders were about to get into a no-holds-barred brawl. Apparently the family atmosphere was over. "Okay, enough," he said. "Jesus. Wade, you haven't even *got* any information yet, so don't go getting worked up about who you're going to share it with. And Kay? I'm going to assume you're talking to me as my friend, because it would be pretty damn unprofessional for my boss to say any of that with a civilian in the room. So, as my friend—thank you. I hear you. Now, let's get back to work."

Kayla frowned at him. "Goddamn it, Jericho . . ." But she didn't go any further. Instead, she jerked to her feet and turned to stare at Wade. "If that's all you've got for the moment, I'll show you out."

Wade smiled peacefully up at her. "You're like a momma bear, aren't you? Growly and fierce, protecting your cub."

"Wade," Jericho said firmly. "Did you have anything else to tell us?"

Wade stood and stretched languorously. "Not right now. But I'll get in touch when I have something more." He smiled at Kayla and said, "I'll be dealing with Jericho. But if you ask nicely enough, maybe we'll let you watch."

"Okay," Jericho said quickly. It was already too late to find a more professional outcome, had probably been too late when he asked Kayla to join them, or when he came back to Mosely, or, hell, when he was born. But he wasn't quite ready to give up on appearances entirely. "Thanks for coming in, Wade. I do appreciate the information."

And then, in a sign that a true compromise was reached, Wade and Kayla both left unsatisfied. Jericho sank back into his desk chair. Wade was being annoying, but had something important to offer. Kayla was suspicious and reluctant, but couldn't completely shut Wade down. And Jericho? Jericho was stuck in the middle. Just another damn day in Mosely, Montana.

CHAPTER 12

Jericho spent the rest of the morning making phone calls to Ohio. He didn't know how the department paid for long distance, but he was probably putting the system to the test, and without getting any real results. Anne Wooderson no longer lived at her address in Akron, Ohio, or anywhere else in the area; the principal of Jefferson Lake Elementary School was the only person who could speak about past students, and she was out of the building for several days; and no one at the Akron PD seemed to have any interest in Keith Wooderson. Jericho did a search of unsolved murders in the city, focusing on those involving prostitutes, but nothing jumped out at him.

He sat at his desk, staring at the computer keyboard, willing the letters to form into some recognizable message. Then he laid his fingers on the keys, and instead of searching the unsolved murders in Akron, he looked at the solved murders. And just like that, he found a match.

Melanie McKay, thirty-six years old, known prostitute and addict. Suspect Jared Scott, thirty-four years old, severe cognitive delays. Committed suicide while awaiting trial. Case closed. Detective Angela Fernandez had taken the lead on the case.

Jericho was dialing the phone before he'd made the conscious decision to move. Goddamn it, there was a pattern. Not only the victim of the murder, but the victim of the framing, as well. *Maybe it's a coincidence, don't get too excited.* But he ignored his inner voice, just like he always seemed to. He had enough real people bitching at him; he didn't need to pay any extra attention to one more voice.

"It's Under-sheriff Jericho Crewe calling from Mosely, Montana. Yes, again. I'm hoping to speak to Detective Fernandez, if she's available?"

He waited through the grumbling on the other end of the line. Possibly he'd been a little impatient earlier, and now karma was paying him back. But he eventually was put through, and a female voice barked, "Detective Fernandez," in his ear.

He was suddenly—not shy, exactly, but hesitant. It had all seemed so clear before he dialed the phone, but now he was struck with self-doubt. What did he have, really? A prostitute victim and an intellectually disabled suspect? Both groups were represented at higher than usual rates in the criminal justice system. Two points weren't enough to make a pattern; it was probably just a coincidence.

But he thought of Will, withdrawn and confused in the holding cells. "My name's Jericho Crewe. I'm an under-sheriff in Mosely, Montana, and I'm working a case where I'm seeing some parallels to the Melanie McKay murder. Do you have a few minutes to talk to me about that?"

The pause was too long before Detective Fernandez quietly said, "Jesus Christ. Shit." Then, after another pause, "He did it again. The fucker did it again."

Jericho's chest tightened. He'd been expecting another dead end, he realized. "Maybe," he said carefully. "Who are you referring to?"

"Wooderson." She spat the name like an obscenity. "Is that who you're calling me about?"

"Keith Wooderson," Jericho agreed, almost dizzy. "I have no proof, yet, but I'm looking at him in connection with a case that sounds a lot like yours. Prostitute murdered, clear evidence pointing to an intellectually disabled perp. But something doesn't feel right. Jesus Christ, this was a long shot, calling you. Chasing him down at all. I thought he was just—just another asshole. But there's more?"

"Where did you say you were calling from?" She sounded tired, but determined. "We should sit down."

"I'm in Mosely, Montana. It's a full day's drive from Ohio."

"What's the nearest airport?"

"You might get a flight into Kalispell, but it's more likely to be Bozeman. And we're four or five hours from there."

"Give me your information. I'm going to try to get a flight, and then I'll call you back."

Damn, this woman didn't mess around. "Your department wants him that bad? They're going to pay for this?"

"My department thinks the case is solved and closed. *I'm* going to pay for this." A pause before she muttered, "I've been paying for it for over a year now."

There wasn't much else to say. Jericho gave her the contact information, then went to update his boss. But when he opened Kayla's office door and saw her standing in the middle of the room, the expression on her face stopped him short.

"Shit, Kay, what's wrong?"

She wasn't crying, but it might have been easier to handle if she was. Instead, she looked . . . shocked, maybe. Dead, more like it. The light that usually animated her, the passion and enthusiasm that drove her, was completely gone.

He stepped toward her, and she stepped back, her hand out to hold him away. As if he could ever seem like a threat to Kayla.

"What happened?" he whispered. She seemed physically okay herself, and had no kids, no siblings. Two ex-husbands she generally just shook her head about. The only person she was really close to was— "Your dad? Is this about your dad?"

Her eyes widened. "You knew?"

"What?" Oh shit, this was about the corruption. "No, I thought—I don't know, I thought he had a heart attack or something. But—"

"But you *did* know," she said, her eyes wide and searching. This time, she was the one moving forward and he was the one tempted to move away. "You *knew*, and you didn't tell me?"

"Slow down, Kay. I'm not sure what you're talking about, and I want to be on the same page, having the same conversation. What are you upset about?"

"He's been passing on information," she said, snarling like it had been *Jericho* who'd betrayed her. "I'd tell him things—he's the ex-sheriff, we're *trained* to talk to retired cops when we need advice, and he's— Jesus, Jericho, he's my *dad*." She still wasn't crying, but her face was twisted and broken. "Why would he do that to me?"

"Shit," Jericho said, and this time when he moved forward, she let him, let him wrap his arms around her and hold her up as she sagged into him. "I'm so sorry, Kay, I don't know why he did it."

She took comfort for about four ragged, sobbing breaths, then roughly shoved him away. "But you knew he *was* doing it, and you didn't tell me!"

"Yeah." He wanted to explain, but he was worried it would sound too much like making excuses, and he didn't want to do that. "I wish I could have told you. I'm sorry."

She turned away, staring out the window of her office onto the bright, sunny street. "I had to find out from Wade fucking Granger."

"Wade told you?"

"Oh, not in so many words," she said bitterly. "But he knew what he was doing. I tried to get in the way of him getting what he wanted, so he had to hurt me. Had to punish me, right?"

Jesus, Jericho hoped that wasn't true. Wade was lot of things, but Jericho wouldn't have said he was deliberately cruel. "What'd he say, exactly?"

"He—" Her voice wavered, and she took a deep breath, shook her head impatiently, then exhaled. She took a new breath and sounded calmer, at least on the surface. "When I walked him out, I asked him why he came to the office instead of your apartment. I accused him of advertising, putting on a show. And he said from what he heard, he had an audience wherever he went, so why shouldn't he play to the bigger crowd? He knew the feds were tailing him, and he wanted me to wonder *how* he knew."

"But I could have told him about the feds tailing him. I didn't, but I could have."

"That's what I thought had happened. I got mad at him for corrupting you, said that you telling him that showed that he was dragging you down. And that's when he said you hadn't told him. So I asked him how he knew, and he just smiled that fucking *evil* smile of his and said, 'I heard it from the sheriff, Sheriff.' It took me a while to figure out what he meant, to be honest." She smiled as if in fond memory of the more naïve woman she'd been earlier in the day. "I came up here and tried to forget about it, then I thought maybe I should have my office swept for bugs or something, and then a few minutes ago it hit me. The feds shutting me out—" She spun toward Jericho, fierce and almost wild. "They know, don't they? That's why they stopped trusting me with information. They knew I'd talk to my dad about it, and he'd pass it along to— Jesus, Jay, who was he talking to? Only Wade? And *why*? For *money*? Or just because he doesn't like the feds and wanted to screw them over? Why the hell would he do this to me, Jay?"

"I don't know. Maybe it's not really about you, you know? I mean, I hope it isn't. Maybe he hasn't thought it through, hasn't realized that what he's doing could hurt you."

"How could he not realize that?"

"I guess he thinks he won't get caught. I mean, criminals—" He caught himself. Maybe that wasn't the word he should be using to refer to Kayla's dad. But the damage had already been done, so he continued. "They never think they're going to get caught, right? So if he never gets caught, then you'll never get in trouble and he's not hurting you. Is that possible?"

"You're being more generous than I'd expect you to be." She shook her head. "All this time I've been nagging at you about Wade, and *I'm* the one who's been letting my personal life get in the way of my work. *I'm* the one who's been compromised."

"But you didn't know. Whatever stupid shit I'm doing with Wade, I'm doing it with my eyes open. You couldn't have been expected to know about your dad."

"But *you* found out about it," she said softly. "How? Wade told you?"

And another damn land mine appeared. His mind raced. She already knew the feds knew about her dad. Was there any harm in telling her the whole story? Hopefully not, because he was going to do it. "Hockley told me. He wanted me on board because he was trying to keep you from getting dragged into it all. At least, that was his story. He wanted me to be aware of the situation so I'd do what he wanted if he needed me to—I don't know, he wasn't crystal clear. But it seemed like he wanted an ally who'd move fast if he saw an opportunity to protect you from the fallout."

"That's pretty fucking paternalistic," she growled.

He managed to bite his tongue and not mention that given the way her actual *pater* was behaving, it seemed like being protective wasn't paternalistic at all. "We were looking out for a colleague," he said.

"Oh, yeah, 'colleagues.' I guess it's just a coincidence that both of you are my ex-lovers?"

"You slept with *Hockley*?"

"What, he didn't mention that when you guys were talking about me behind my back?"

"Chill out, Kay. Our intentions were good—at least, mine were." He grimaced. "*Hockley*? Jesus, that's— I can only assume your taste in men has changed a lot since high school if you find *him* attractive."

"Yeah, I like straight guys now. Why the hell are we talking about this?"

"I have no idea. You brought it up, and I haven't been able to burn it out of my memory yet."

She snorted, and he felt better. She wasn't going to fall apart, not all the way. Not so far that she wouldn't be able to pull herself back together, especially if she had a little help from her friends. So he said, "We should talk to him, maybe. Hockley. He's not in tight with the investigation—"

"They're investigating my dad? There's a formal investigation?"

"Well, shit, Kay, they aren't going to just ignore it if they find a corrupt sheriff, even if he's retired. Yeah, they're investigating. But the FBI, not the DEA. Hockley's not cool enough to be FBI, so he's not really in on the details. We could talk to him, see what he can tell us. Figure out your next step."

"I'm pretty sure my next step involves going over to my dad's place and burning his fucking house down."

"We should give Wade a call. He's got a real gift for arson."

Another snort, but then she shook her head. "No. I'm not going to fucking laugh about this. Not about anything distantly related to this. Stop trying to make me feel better—I want to feel bad."

"Okay. Hey, are those pants getting a bit tight? I think maybe you're putting on weight."

She smacked his shoulder, hard. "I want to feel bad about my dad, not feel bad in general."

"Right. Got it." He was quiet for a moment, then said, "Want me to go find Hockley?"

"In a minute," she said. "For now, though, can you—can you just sit over there and be quiet, and let me catch up to all the ways my life just fell apart?"

"You want me to go back to my office? I can give you some space."

"No. I want you to stay. But I need you to shut up, okay?"

He didn't answer, just went over and sat in the chair and let her regroup. She was Kay. She was tough. She'd get past this and come out swinging. And if she decided her next step involved flames, Jericho would help her pour the gasoline.

CHAPTER 13

"**W**hy the fuck did you tell her?" Hockley hissed. They were standing by the station's front door, where Jericho had caught Hockley on his way in from lunch.

"I didn't tell her," Jericho said after pulling Hockley out the door and into a more private spot in the parking lot. "She got a hint from Wade, and then worked it out herself. The main clue was that you all stopped giving her information, if you want to know the truth."

"Wade Granger? Why is he involved?"

"I think you're focusing on the wrong stuff here. Kay knows, she's pissed at—well, pretty much everyone, but definitely you, me, and her dad. She's looking to bust some heads. If you want to manage the situation before it explodes, this is your chance."

"It's *always* right to focus on Granger. He's the source of all problems in this goddamn town."

"You're upset," Jericho said with exaggerated kindness, "and it's making you extra-specially dramatic. I understand. And, honestly, I don't really give a shit if Kayla goes over and reams her dad out and blows the FBI's whole case out of the water. I think it'd be good for her, and I don't have the same jones for punishing the old guy that you do, so—okay, sure, let's talk about Wade some more. That'll be nice." He smiled. "I mean, it makes sense for you and me to be friends. We have so much in common, since *both* of us seem to form inappropriate attachments to people under federal investigation."

That rocked Hockley back for a couple of seconds, at least. Then he said lamely, "We're investigating her *father*. She's just—"

"Collateral damage?"

"Goddamn it," Hockley said, but he seemed to be talking about the whole situation, not Jericho's contributions in particular. "Okay, yeah, I need to talk to her and figure out how to get in front of this. Can you—"

"Come with you and see what she wants me to do? Sure."

"I was thinking more along the lines of staying out of it and keeping your mouth shut—" He saw Jericho's expression and shrugged. "But, sure, coming along and helping out is good too."

So Jericho tagged along, and it was nice to watch Kayla directing a portion of her anger in Hockley's direction. But after that burned off, she was back to looking hurt and betrayed, and that was *not* how he wanted to see her.

"He didn't want me to run for sheriff," she said as she stared out the window. "Didn't want me to be a cop at all. He said it was because he worried about my safety, but I don't know, it kind of felt like he thought I wasn't tough enough to do it. So if he screws my career up like this, then he ends up being right, doesn't he? I *couldn't* handle the job."

"You know I'm not a big fan of your dad," Jericho said, "but I honestly don't think he's *that* much of an asshole. Do you?" She didn't answer, so he continued. "I think he's probably just arrogant. He assumed he wouldn't get caught. And it seems like the bikers aren't talking, at least so far—" He cut his gaze toward Hockley, who was taking his own turn staring pointedly out the window, and groaned. "Shit. The bikers *are* talking. They'd be stupid not to, if they thought they could use their testimony to make a better deal. But the feds haven't moved in yet, haven't busted him, so he thinks the bikers kept their mouths shut. He thinks he's untouchable."

"Is that true?" Kayla demanded of Hockley. "Was he selling information to the bikers? Are they going to testify against him?"

"I don't know," Hockley said. "I asked the FBI to take me out of the loop for this case. Montgomery's working as liason with them, and he's going to tell me anything I need to know." He gave Kayla a defiant look. "Anything I need to know to help *you* stay out of trouble. Not your father. There's nothing I can do for him, and even if there was, I wouldn't do it."

"What am *I* supposed to do now that I know?" The question was clearly rhetorical. Kayla had turned away from the window and was pacing like a caged lion. Jericho wanted to be sure he wasn't in mauling range when she burst out from behind the bars. "Do I seriously pretend I'm in the dark? I don't warn him, don't yell at him—I go on like none of this is happening? Is that what I'm expected to do?"

"It's a difficult situation," Hockley said unhelpfully.

Jericho tried to do better. "It's too late to help your dad. I mean, if the feds were pretty sure they had him *before* the bikers turned—assuming they did, which I think is a good assumption—then they've got an even tighter case, now. The big question is what they're waiting for. Why haven't they busted him yet?"

"No rush," Kayla said bitterly. "They've stopped telling me anything, so none of *their* information is being leaked. And they don't give a shit about *my* cases. They got a bunch of good press from busting the bikers, so they can afford to sit on this and wait until they need some positive attention. There's really only Wade left to be buying information, anyway."

Wade. "Are they trying to use your dad to catch Wade?" Jericho asked. Shit, it made sense. "But he knows they know about your dad. I don't know how, but he wouldn't have told you about this if he thought it was going to mess up a valuable source of information for himself. They're not going to get Wade that easily."

"Easily?" Hockley said with a raised eyebrow. "We've been working on the bastard for the better part of the year. One man against the DEA *and* FBI, but the slippery bastard hasn't given us enough for a jaywalking ticket, let alone a federal conviction. There's been nothing easy about it."

Jericho wanted to suggest that maybe Wade wasn't actually committing any crimes and the whole thing had been a big misunderstanding, but out of respect for Kayla's state of mind, he restrained himself. "It's bad, Kay," he said instead. "And I know this isn't what you need to hear right now, but we have another problem. I don't have details yet, but I talked to a detective who worked a case similar to Lorraine's in Ohio, where Keith Wooderson used to live. She gave me his name, no prompting, as soon as she heard the details of our case. She's coming here, on her own dime." He glanced over at Hockley, then back at Kayla. "We might be facing a serial killer here. And if we get any confirmation from this detective when she arrives, we need to cut Will Archer loose. There's too much evidence suggesting he was framed."

"Jesus Christ." Kayla took a deep breath. "I should step down. At least temporarily. This department has important work to do, and I can't let my personal stuff get in the way of that."

"Kay, if you step down, *I'm* next in line to take over. You honestly think that'd make things any better?"

She stared at him, then snorted and turned to Hockley. "You must think we're a bit of a mess."

He shook his head. "It's a small town. I'm learning what that means. Relationships aren't as black and white up here. In the city, cops can stay away from criminals. Up here, they might have gone to school with you, live next door to you, be related to you, whatever. It's not a mess, it's just different."

Again, Jericho had to resist the urge to make a smart comment about Hockley's own recent exploration of close small-town relationships. Hockley deserved to take some shit, but Kay needed Jericho to be solid right then, not stirring things up for his own amusement and revenge.

"Can you talk to the FBI?" he suggested to Kayla. "I mean—if you did talk to them, could you tell them what they're going to want to hear? Can you keep your cool and not tell your dad what's going on?"

Her eyes were wide. "He's my *dad*, Jay. This is my job, and it's important to me, but he's my *dad*."

"Then you can't talk to the FBI," Hockley said quickly. "You can't tell them that. As understandable as it is, if you tell them that, they'll look at you for interfering with their investigation, at the best. They could try for conspiracy charges, or—I don't know what they'll come up with. But if you can't be completely on their side, you need them to believe you're in the dark." He frowned. "Who else knows about this so far?"

"Who else knows that Kay knows?" Jericho said. "Just this room and Wade."

"Granger's not going to share his information with the FBI. He recited the alphabet for five hours straight the last time they hauled him in." There might almost have been respect in Hockley's tone, however grudging. "He was doing different voices, dialects, dramatic interpretations, everything. Just the ABCs." He raised his eyebrows at Jericho. "I can see what the two of you have in common."

"Besides liking dick," Jericho said. Yeah, it was childish, but he'd been restraining himself for too long, and this wasn't something that was going to hurt Kay.

Hockley straightened his shoulders. "So what's the plan? Kayla, I guess this is up to you. Do you need to take some time to sort it out, and then you can talk to me or Jericho about it? Both of us, maybe, and we can try to run interference for you. Whatever you decide you need to do."

"No," Jericho said. He was pretty sure he was on the right track. At least he hoped he was. "We can't sit on this. Kay, if you don't talk to your dad, he'll know something's up. And if you *do* talk to him, you're screwed either way—if you talk about your cases, you're *knowingly* sharing intel with a leak, and if you don't talk about them, he'll want to know why, and the feds could accuse you of tipping him off about the investigation. You could feed him fake intel, but that won't last long before he figures it out, not if you don't mix some real stuff in with the fake." Yeah, that was the problem, and he hoped he had the solution. "You two should stay here. Or go talk to people or whatever, but no phone calls. Nothing that could give the appearance of you spilling information." He stared at Hockley, willing the man to understand, and saw that he did.

Unfortunately, so did Kayla. "No way. This isn't your fight! You can't get involved in it. You have a career to worry about too."

But he'd already decided. "I'm just a future burnout, right? I'm not going back to LA." He'd said it as a joke but realized that it was true. He had no idea what his future held, but it wasn't going to be anything like his past. "This town needs you. It doesn't need me. And, of course, there's the added advantage of me not giving a shit." He grinned at her. "That's always been what slowed you down."

"Jay—" she said, warning clear in her voice. "This is cowboy bullshit again."

"Yeah, a cowboy. Maybe that'll be my next career. Thanks for the suggestion!" She was still frowning, though, so he smiled. "Don't worry, I'm not throwing myself on a grenade. I think there's a path around all that. So while I'm gone, stay off the phone. Go hang out with the feds if you can put up with them. You're here. You're innocent." He looked at Hockley. "You've got a witness."

Hockley nodded. "She does."

Jericho was on his way to the door when he turned back and gave the DEA agent a hard look. "Was this your plan all along? Getting me to do this?" He didn't really expect an answer, and Hockley didn't give him one. So he headed out the door. Maybe he'd been set up and manipulated. Again. Maybe he should just sit back and get used to it, since it seemed as if everyone else in the damn universe was smarter than he was and could plan everything out far into the future.

He couldn't worry about that stuff right then. He had a goal, a mission, and he needed to ensure its success. He'd worry about the rest of it when he was back at base. Or never. Maybe he'd worry about it never. That had a nice ring to it.

CHAPTER 14

It felt good to be doing something. Of course, that instinct toward action instead of reflection had gotten Jericho in trouble plenty of times in the past, but he was reasonably confident he was doing the right thing this time.

He pulled his car into a parking spot on Main Street. His own car, not the department cruiser; it seemed important to draw as many lines between himself and his job as he could on this one. He thought about ditching at least a few pieces of his uniform, but considering who he was meeting, it was probably best to remain fully clothed.

He knew that had been a good decision as soon as he saw Wade's lazy sprawl in the diner's back booth and felt the stirring in his own gut, and a little lower. More clothes were definitely a good thing in this case.

"Under-sheriff," Wade said with an oily smile as Jericho approached. "Imagine my surprise when you called me. *Pleasant* surprise, naturally, but I was under the impression that your boss wanted communications to go through her? You're being defiant so soon?"

"Stop it." Jericho turned his cup over so the server could pour him coffee he didn't want, then waved off her question about food. After she'd gone back to the kitchen he said, "You made a hell of a mess today. You need to help me clean it up."

"I don't think *I* made that mess. Was I the one selling out his daughter for a few bucks? Was that me?"

"You're the one who told her about it. Hockley and I were trying to handle it quietly, but you screwed that up."

"You and Hockley. How sweet. I wasn't aware the two of you were friends."

"Jesus, Wade, you sound jealous."

"Don't be silly. I have it on good authority that you're not his type, even though he does seem to like the uniform."

"Where the hell did you get *that* from?" Jericho wasn't sure whether to be amazed or appalled at Wade's information gathering. "Not from Kay's dad, I hope." And, yeah, *that* was what they were supposed to be talking about. "Does he know you told Kay about him? Does he know the feds are after him?"

"I can't really say what someone else knows, can I?"

"Did you tell him anything about it?"

"That's generally not the direction information flows between he and I."

"Have you ever in your life just said yes or no to a single goddamn question without being forced into it?"

"No," Wade said, and then he grinned. Goddamn it, Jericho had been doing okay until the grin. But that one little gesture, the tiny twitch of lips Jericho knew so well and wanted to know so much better—

"I need you to tell him about the feds," Jericho said. He had to control himself and stay on topic. "You've obviously got some way of communicating with him that the feds don't know about. I need you to talk to him."

Wade cocked his head. "You're asking me to commit a crime. You're suggesting that I should interfere with a federal investigation."

"Yeah. I am."

"Because you'd rather I get caught than precious Kayla get caught for doing the same damn thing?"

"Because you *won't* get caught. You're good at this stuff; Kay's good at the other side of things. And you don't have a motive, but she does. If Donald Morgan suddenly changes his behavior, the feds are going to look at Kay, not at you."

"The feds look at what I have for breakfast. They're looking at us having this meeting at this moment. They can't hear anything, as far as I know, but that doesn't mean they don't know it's happening." He shook his head. "You're asking me to take a risk, and there's no reason for me to do it. Telling Morgan about the feds does me no good. So why should I do it?"

"Why'd you tell Kay about it this morning? She thinks you were pissy and trying to hurt her, but I don't believe that. So you had some other motive for doing it, and all these arguments you're making are just your way of covering up your real reasons. But if Kay's right, and you *were* simply trying to get back at her? Then you should help clean up the mess, because that's not the kind of person you are; you don't go out of your way to hurt other people just because you're in a bad mood."

Wade was quiet for a few moments, then said, "You truly think that? You think I'm not that kind of person? What exactly are you basing that opinion on?"

Jericho frowned. "I'm basing it on . . . I don't know, on *you*. On knowing you. You're not cruel, Wade. You never have been. If I'm wrong about that?" Jesus, what did it mean if he was wrong about that? "If I'm wrong about that, I'm wrong about pretty much everything else I believe too. If I don't know that about you, then I guess I don't know much of anything."

"You must be aware that the vast majority of people we know would disagree with you entirely."

"You must be aware that I don't give a shit about the opinions of the vast majority of people we know."

"You're reverting, Jay." Wade leaned back in the booth and laced his fingers behind his head. "You got a bit tight when you were away, got all caught up in the rules and the proper way to do things. But you're loosening up. Your Crewe blood is coming out, in a good way."

"I wasn't aware there *was* a good way for Crewe blood to come out."

"Hell yeah, there is." Wade sounded like he really meant it. "Your old man had a mean streak, and you probably got hit with the worst of it from him. I know that. But he had some strengths too. He was tough, loyal, smart, independent—your family's been living up here in the woods since before this was even a state, and they didn't survive because they were *weak*. Not at all."

"You seem a bit evangelical about it."

"The Church of the Holy Crewe," Wade said. "I've always been a devout member, more than ready to worship." His smile now was slow and seductive and pulled at Jericho, mind, body, and soul.

Jericho tried to resist. "We're off topic again. I need you to tell Donald Morgan about the feds."

"Because if he already knows about them, then Kayla can't get in trouble for spilling the beans. And because Kayla's not going to be feeding him any more information anyway, so it's not going to hurt the feds' case if he knows they're looking at him."

"Exactly. And it's not going to hurt you, either, since you're not going to get anything from him anymore."

Wade looked thoughtful. "And if I decide not to do it? What then?"

Jericho shrugged. He wasn't sure why he didn't want to say it. Maybe everything would be simpler if they kept things on the terms they were currently on.

But Wade had never cared much about keeping things simple. "If I don't tell him, you're going to," he said slowly. "Right? You've got to be the white knight, riding in to save the fair maiden. You can't just let this take care of itself."

"If you don't tell him, I'll figure something else out."

"You'll risk your damn career, risk getting charged with a federal offense. That's what you'll do."

"Probably," Jericho finally conceded.

Wade nodded. "Okay. So, fine, I'll take care of it. But not because of the kind of person I am or you believe I am. Not because of Kayla Morgan, or some loyalty you seem to think I might feel toward her. I'll do it for you, Jay. And all I want in return?"

Jericho braced himself.

"I just want you to acknowledge it. I want you to *know* I'm doing it for you. I want you to admit that—to me and to yourself."

What game was Wade playing? What were the rules, and how the hell did he think either of them could ever win it? The smart thing would be to refuse to play. But instead, Jericho nodded. "I'd appreciate it if you'd do this for me, Wade."

Wade smiled, and it left Jericho feeling as if he'd just signed a deal with the devil, and not regretting it one bit.

Doubt began to creep in as Jericho drove back to the office, but he dismissed it. Yes, he'd just asked a known criminal to interfere with a federal investigation on his behalf. It had happened, and now it was done with. There was no way to change it and therefore no point worrying about it, not when there was so much more going on.

More being a possible serial killer. One who framed disabled, vulnerable people to take the fall for his crimes. Ugly, but smart. Will was physically strong, completely able to have committed the crime, but didn't have the mental resources to defend himself from prosecution. He wouldn't be able to convince anyone that he was innocent. Which meant he needed someone else to do that for him.

When Jericho got back to the station, he detoured around to the cells at the side where Will was being held. The judge hadn't set the bail all that high, but it was high enough that Will couldn't pay it, and no relatives were paying, either. Jericho had heard rumors of the Applebys trying to mortgage the hardware store to raise money, but the truth was the place wasn't worth much. No, it wasn't likely that Will would be getting bailed out, so Jericho needed to hurry up and find another way for him to be freed.

In the meantime, though, he crouched down outside the bars of the cell and waited to be noticed. Will was sitting on the thin mattress, rocking a little, staring at the wall. Shit, he didn't look good. This whole thing had to be incredibly stressful for him: finding the body, the arrest, being held somewhere unfamiliar. Pretty damn frightening—all of it.

"Will," Jericho said gently. "Hey, Will, it's me. Jericho. We went to school together. I'm your friend, okay?"

There was no response.

"We're going to try to get you out of there, Will. As soon as we can, I promise."

Still nothing.

"I saw in the visitor book that Mr. and Mrs. Appleby have been coming to see you." He didn't mention the other visitor, didn't want to think about Will, trapped behind bars while Wooderson taunted him. "The Applebys are nice people, aren't they? And it's good that you work at the hardware store—they're not as young as they used to be, and I'm sure they need your help. So we'll get you back to that as soon as we can."

He shifted around so he was sitting rather than crouching, and stayed there awhile longer. He didn't have anything to say, but it just didn't seem right to cut the visit too short. Besides, it gave him time to think.

At first, of course, his mind went to Wade. He was out there doing something illegal. Doing it for Jericho. If he got caught, he'd be in trouble because of Jericho. Was that all Wade's request had been about? Had he just been setting up a big guilt trip?

No. It had been more than that. A declaration, although what was being declared was hard to pin down. Nothing with Wade could ever be simple. But hopefully the problem with Kayla was—not resolved, but tidied up. Jericho couldn't do anything to keep her dad from being dirty, and he damn well wouldn't do anything to keep the old bastard from getting caught. But tipping him off now, when his pipeline of information had already dried up? Jericho was okay with that.

Will moved in his cell, just shuffled an inch or so along the bed, and Jericho watched him for a moment. Then he remembered Keith Wooderson, and frowned. What kind of asshole— Well, shit. The man had beaten a couple of women to death, and Jericho was surprised that he'd been evil enough to frame an innocent for it? That was stupid.

"Keith Wooderson," Jericho said gently, experimentally. "Mr. Wooderson, the man from the alley. Do you know him, Will? He came to see you here too. Do you know Mr. Wooderson?"

There was no response. Maybe he should let it go. What was he trying to prove? He already believed Will was innocent, and it wasn't like he was going to get any useful information out of the man. But still, he kept talking. "Tux. Tuxedo—was that his full name? I heard he was a nice cat."

And Will stopped rocking. He didn't make eye contact, but for the first time he seemed to be listening. Like he was connecting with Jericho's words. The social worker had said Will's receptive language abilities were much higher than his expressive. He could understand, as long as he paid attention.

"Something bad happened to Tux. I'm really sorry about that. Something bad happened to Lorraine too. I'm sorry we couldn't stop it. I wish we'd—" What? What did he wish? "I wish we'd known there was a bad man living here. Then we could have tried to stop him, or warned people. I'm sorry we didn't know, Will. I'm really sorry."

They sat together for a while until Will started rocking again, and Jericho climbed to his feet. "I'll see you later, Will. We're going to do what we can to make things better. I promise."

He left the holding area and was halfway up the stairs to his office when he stopped, then turned around and went back to find the officer in charge of the cells. "I want a suicide watch on Will Archer," he said. "I don't know if he's got the ability to hurt himself in there, but I want to be sure it doesn't happen. And if anyone but the Applebys come to visit, contact me or the sheriff right away. And can you let people know—" What? That arresting Will had been a mistake? Yeah, he'd own that mistake if it got Will better treatment. But he just said, "Let everyone know we're a long way from sure that he's guilty. He needs to be treated gently. Keep yourselves safe, but as much as you can, make this okay for him."

The officer was clearly doubtful, which made sense. Just how okay could things be for someone locked up in an eight-by-eight cell? But he nodded his agreement, and Jericho went upstairs feeling a bit better.

He was standing in the central office area when the feds began to swarm at the far end of the room. They were agitated about something, obviously, and Jericho hoped he knew what it was.

Hockley came out, Kayla at his heels, and they both turned to Jericho, who shrugged back at them. "They didn't bring you in on whatever it is?" he asked Hockley.

"This is exclusively FBI. They're not including DEA."

Jericho nodded, and tried not to let Kayla see him sneaking a concerned glance at her. She looked strained, but not as close to the edge as she'd been earlier. That was good, surely.

No one did much for a couple of minutes, but then one of the agents broke away from the pack and approached. "Sheriff Morgan," he said awkwardly. "We have a suspect coming in, and we're going to need to use one of your interrogation rooms."

"What suspect?" she demanded. She sounded a little brittle, maybe, but under control.

The agent grimaced. "We've just been contacted by former Sheriff Donald Morgan. He's apparently aware that we're investigating him for some . . . irregularities during his time in this office, and he's volunteered to come in with his lawyer to get things cleared up. This is a preliminary meeting, but we'll want it recorded."

"'Irregularities'? What does that mean, exactly?"

"I'm sorry, but I can't discuss that with you. You understand that this is a delicate situation, of course." He took a deep breath. "And just as a professional courtesy, I should tell you—we're going to want to speak to you about these issues as well."

"I see." Maybe she'd have added something more, but that was when her father appeared at the top of the stairs, a gray-suited man trailing behind him. The man in the suit seemed a little flustered, which made sense considering how quickly all this was happening, but Donald Morgan seemed completely, arrogantly relaxed. He looked exactly how Wade always looked when *he* was brought in for questioning, but Jericho doubted either of the men would appreciate hearing that comparison made out loud.

The FBI agent turned and gestured Morgan toward one of the interrogation rooms, and Kayla stood like a soldier as her father walked past her with only a cursory nod.

Before the interrogation room door closed, Kayla turned and headed into her own office, Jericho and Hockley trailing behind her.

"This will be quick," Jericho said, hoping he was right. "They're just establishing contact. Making it clear they know about the investigation as of today. So if the feds can't prove you told him about it before today—which they can't, since you didn't know about it— then they can't accuse you of obstructing justice or tipping him off."

"They can accuse me of giving him a hell of a lot of other information over the years," she said dully.

"But you said it yourself," Hockley interjected. "You're *trained* to consult with the people who held your office before you. You're *supposed* to talk to others and assume you can trust them. The FBI can't blame you for doing what you were expected to do."

"It's not only the FBI to worry about," Kayla said dully. "This is an elected position, and this town is sick of corrupt cops. If the voters think I'm crooked, or naïve and stupid, trusting someone I shouldn't have—" She grimaced. "You know Jackson's soaking all this in, looking for his chance to make his move. He's a fucking awful deputy, but he'd be even worse as sheriff."

"Worry about that later," Jericho suggested. "We have no idea how this is going to play out. Today's victory was making sure there were no criminal charges against you; tomorrow we can worry about getting you reelected."

And worry about helping Will and stopping Keith Wooderson. And working through how he felt about Eli, and Nikki and the kids, and every other messy thing in his damn life. But for the moment, he was satisfied. Wade had come through. He'd gotten the message to Donald Morgan, and somehow, either because of Wade or because Morgan had a conscience and had realized how badly this could hurt his daughter, the old man had done the one right thing that was left for him to do.

At least one damn part of all this was coming together.

CHAPTER 15

Angela Fernandez arrived at the station early the next morning. She had salt-and-pepper hair and frown lines so deep they made it seem like her nose extended up into her forehead. After Jericho introduced himself, she gave him a long look up and down and clearly found no reason to be impressed.

"What have you got on him?" she grunted.

"Come on upstairs. Can I get you coffee or anything? You must be tired after the flight and that long drive. Have you had breakfast?" Jericho wasn't sure why he was trying to be charming. Probably just his usual instinct to do whatever would irritate someone the most.

And based on the scowl he received as they climbed to the upper floor, his efforts were paying off. "You can get me the file on this case and somewhere to read it over. That's all I need."

"The file won't tell you that much. I've got my notes, but they're not typed up yet—they're still preliminary. I'm operating mostly on instinct, here. Not a lot of evidence."

"No evidence at all?" she asked skeptically as she trudged up the stairs.

"There's lots of evidence pointing toward the guy we've got locked up for the crime. But nothing to indicate Wooderson is involved."

"So why the hell did you call me? Why'd you drive the sergeant at the station crazy with your questions if you don't have any damn evidence?"

"I told you. Instinct. And you flying all the way up here suggests my instinct is right, doesn't it?"

"Instinct won't put the bastard behind bars where he belongs."

"*Our* case is still open. *We're* still investigating." *Nice. Give up the charm offensive in favor of petty sniping.*

Fernandez seemed as unimpressed by the new approach as she'd been by the old. "You must be looking really hard if you've got somebody else already charged with the crime."

"Well, our innocent guy hasn't killed himself yet, so we're still doing better than you guys managed." *Shit. Way too far.*

He wouldn't have thought it possible for her frown lines to get deeper, but he'd have been wrong. "Cut the shit and tell me what you've got," she ordered, and sank into the chair he offered in his office.

Jericho ran through it all, and Fernandez nodded at the appropriate spots—the initial assumptions, the growing evidence, the misgivings. It was a relief to be talking to someone who didn't need to be convinced there was deception going on, and her attitude toward him seemed to improve as they spoke.

"Did he do anything like that in your case?" he asked after telling her about Tux's fate. "Animal abuse on top of the murder?"

"No. Not that we noticed, at least. Strange for animal mutilation to be an *escalation*," she mused. "Usually it would be the other way around. Start with the animals, build to the humans."

"I think it makes sense in this case." Jericho almost wished he was wrong, but didn't think he was. "I don't think this was about killing a woman. I mean, obviously it was, from our perspective. But for Wooderson? I think it was about Will. He didn't frame Will to cover up the murder he really wanted to commit. He committed murder so he had something he could use to frame Will. And he killed the cat as another way to hurt Will. Again, no evidence for any of this, but my instinct? It says this is about hurting intellectually disabled people, and the prostitutes are getting dragged in because they're easy victims." He felt a bit stupid with so little reason to support his opinion, and finished lamely. "There was just something in his face when we arrested Will. He was so fucking happy. Like, fierce about it. I don't know."

He braced himself, but Fernandez didn't dismiss his theory. "Have you talked to the ex-wife yet?" she asked quietly.

"Haven't been able to get hold of her."

"We can help you with that. She's gone into hiding, more or less, trying to get away from him. But we've asked her to check in periodically, and she does."

"So he was abusive to her?" Frustration flashed through him as he added, "And she still let him take the girls with him?"

"They're not her kids. They're from his first wife, and she never adopted them. He wouldn't let her, she said. And I don't know if you could call him 'abusive,' exactly, but he definitely freaked her out. Nothing she could prove, but, I guess, like you, she was trusting her instincts. He made her feel unsafe. But the point is, I talked to her quite a bit, and got some of his background out of her. Apparently his brother had a developmental delay—a pretty serious one. Died in his teens."

Jericho had to remind himself to breathe. "Suspicious circumstances?"

"Not enough to twig anything when we hadn't seen the pattern forming, but it's worth looking into. I'll go over my notes and get the details, see what I can find."

"What about the first wife?"

"Dead. Cancer, though, nothing suspicious about that one."

"How'd you hook onto him in your case? I mean, you never laid charges against him, so it couldn't have been too much. What makes you so sure he's your guy?"

"At the start, nothing. The case seemed open and closed, just like yours. Wooderson was one of the witnesses we had tying the suspect to the scene. A key witness, really. Without his testimony, we probably never would have laid charges. But he saw—he *said* he saw—the suspect go into the victim's apartment. He *said* he heard raised voices, and he said he saw the perp, Jared Scott, leave about five minutes later with blood on his shirt. We later found the shirt, complete with blood that matched the victim's, in Scott's outdoor trash cans."

Jericho nodded. It would have seemed clear enough, certainly. But it also would have been easy for Wooderson to plant the shirt and make up his testimony. "It was an apartment? But nobody else heard or saw anything? How did Wooderson explain seeing so much? He was just hanging out in the hallway the whole time?"

"It was summer, and the place had bad air conditioning. He said he kept the apartment door open for a cross-breeze, saw it all from his couch."

"And your perp couldn't talk to deny it?"

"He could talk. But he didn't have anything compelling to say. Just a flat-out denial. But he denied other things too. He said he'd never been in the hooker's place, but we had lots of DNA placing him there, he was in her appointment book, and several neighbors, not only Wooderson, had seen him in the building on previous occasions."

"He lied because he was embarrassed about going to a prostitute," Jericho said quietly.

Fernandez nodded. "Seems like. But at the time, we thought he was covering for himself."

Of course they would have. People just didn't frame each other for murder all that often. Even the most paranoid detective would be inclined to take the obvious answer as truth, and not waste a lot of time searching for convoluted alternate theories. "So what changed? What made you think he was involved?"

"He started hounding us. He wasn't aggressive, exactly, but way too involved. He wanted to know every detail of the case, went to visit the suspect in jail, and seemed too wrapped up in it all. I eventually called him on it, and he gave me some line about needing closure in order to get over the trauma of almost witnessing a murder."

"He gave me the closure line too. The girls needed to stick around and see Will come out of the forest because he'd startled them, and they needed to know he was caught, for closure. And he visited Will in jail." Jericho felt almost dirty. He'd been part of it, part of letting this sick bastard get his thrills from watching Will suffer. Now he would damn well be part of making the asshole pay. "Was that it? Just that instinct?"

Fernandez shook her head. "No. Not at all. I kept after him, poking into his background, trying to figure it out, and finally he— well, he confessed, really, but not in a way I could use."

"What do you mean?"

"He didn't actually *say* he did it. But he made it clear all the same, you know? Hinting and smirking about it. He was so fucking proud of himself. I think you're right that framing Jared Scott was part of the thrill, but Wooderson definitely got off on the killing too, and gloating to a cop was the icing on the cake."

"It was reckless, though. Confessing to a cop, even if it's not something admissible in court? That's the kind of ballsy that seems a lot like stupid."

"Not as reckless as you'd think," Fernandez said heavily. "He did it two days after Jared Scott suffocated himself with a trash bag in our lockup facility. We were already taking serious heat for having a guy die in custody; it would have been way, way worse if it had turned out he was innocent."

"So you stopped trying?"

"Fuck you," she shot back at him. Then she frowned, lowered her shoulders, and said, "No, I didn't stop trying. But I was getting no support. The prosecutor, my boss—they wanted this to just go away. There was no family yelling at them, no community concern. Dead whore, dead perp, dead case. You know?" Her voice had the remains of bitterness in it, but also a fair dose of pragmatism. Things were the way they were. "I kept after him when I could. Kept an eye on him and let him know I was watching. But I'm a single person; I couldn't do twenty-four-hour surveillance, and I had other cases to worry about. So one day I went by his house, and he wasn't there. His fucking job is totally mobile—I don't know what it takes to design a website, but he does it all over the internet, with whatever business names he feels like using. He pulled the girls out of school and took a copy of their records with him so nobody'd be calling back to get information on them. He was gone, and it's not like I could initiate a large-scale manhunt with no support from the higher-ups."

"But now he's here, and you are too," Jericho said. "Now we've got a chance to get him for this murder, and maybe others. I mean, we only know about two, but there could be more, right?"

"I did a pretty thorough search of his past. I hadn't figured out the connection to disabled people, so maybe that'll be a new filter that lets me find something new. But it's not catching him for past crimes that I'm worried about. Not really."

Jericho nodded. "Yeah. The most important thing is the future. He's already done this at least twice, each murder ruining two lives, and we don't stop him? We know how serial killers work. If we don't stop him, he'll kill again."

CHAPTER 16

Frustration was part of the job. The gut-churning, the weight that seemed as if it would keep bearing down until it crushed Jericho—or until he did something to shake it off. It felt wrong to do anything for himself when there was so much work to be done, but Jericho knew from experience that his brain wouldn't work when he was so tight, so heavy. He'd found two different ways to address the problem in the past. Now? A night of wild sex was out, given the limited social options in his current location, so he settled for a hard workout. Weights until his arms and legs were trembling and his core muscles were so fried he was nauseous, then a short break before heading out for a run.

Instead of turning up into the mountains as he usually did, he aimed toward town. No real reason for it, just, well, instinct, he supposed. His subconscious mind sending him signals he was too tired to override. As his feet pounded the pavement, he let his thoughts go where they wanted.

Lorraine, with her brutal life and even more brutal death. Keith fucking Wooderson, killing and destroying for his own sick enjoyment. Will, frightened and alone, trapped inside himself as securely as he was trapped in the jail.

Kayla, betrayed by her own father. Hopefully she wasn't facing criminal charges, but her career was at risk, and without her in office, Jackson would sweep in pretty well unopposed. The town would be protected by someone with a greater interest in power than justice.

It was a sign of how twisted his life had gotten that his mind shifted to thinking about Wade as a way to calm down and *stop* feeling conflicted. Wade was complicated, yes. His presence was woven through most of Jericho's other issues, sometimes as a help, sometimes as a hindrance, but Wade himself? Jericho's feelings toward Wade himself were becoming clearer with every stride along the sidewalk.

"I want you to know *I'm doing it for you."* That had been Wade's condition, and Jericho had taken it to heart. Wade had helped Kayla, for Jericho. Wade had risked his life helping to rescue the kids, for Jericho. Wade had done plenty of crazy, manipulative, fucking maddening things too, of course—Wade wasn't a simple person. But Jericho and Wade? Just the two of them, without all the surrounding crap? They were, compared to everything else, shockingly straightforward.

So when he turned around and jogged back through town, it felt natural to cut into the alley that ran behind the Main Street businesses, and when he reached the collection of beat-up cars and parts that was the back of Scotty Hawk's garage, naturally he slowed to a walk, and then stopped completely.

It wasn't like Wade lived there. Jericho actually didn't know where Wade lived, just one of many gaps in his knowledge. But Wade and Scotty did business together, and Scotty reported everything that happened in town to Wade, and Wade was—

Wade was there. Coming out of the back of the shop, slowly, cautiously. Jericho stepped into an alcove between a wrecked cube van and the brick wall of a neighboring business, and Wade followed him.

"What can I do for you today, Under-sheriff?" Wade asked. When Jericho didn't answer, Wade's voice softened. "Jay? What do you need?"

It was all too damn clear, and Wade was right there, right where he'd always been. So Jericho stepped forward, closing the space between them, and it all happened at once. His lips on Wade's, one hand behind his neck and the other at the small of his back, holding them together, the way they should always be.

Wade was pliant at first, then quickly responsive. His fingers tightened in the sweat-soaked fabric of Jericho's shirt, holding on as if Jericho might try to escape. Might stay away for another fifteen damn years.

"I missed you too," Jericho said as soon as he came up for air. "I miss you every time I'm not with you. And you're right, nothing else matters." He was almost desperate, now, and his kiss was harder and deeper than before. Then he pulled away for a moment. "Nothing else makes sense. It's just you and me. Just this."

Another kiss, then Jericho let his mouth trail down, exploring stubbled skin and sharp angles. Wade threw his head back, exposed and vulnerable and trusting, and something powerful surged through Jericho, something beyond want. He *needed* this, needed to claim and possess and protect Wade. And for a brief moment there in the dirty alley, it seemed like Wade was going to let him do all of that.

But then Wade gasped and jerked away from Jericho. "No," he said. "Shit, Jay, what the hell are you doing? There's feds all over me, and we're practically on the goddamn sidewalk!"

"I told you, I don't care. None of that matters."

Wade got his hands up and pushed Jericho away, staggering a few steps to the side as he did it. "*I* care. Because you'll care again soon, once you're past whatever the hell you're thinking at this second, and you'll blame me for dragging you down. Fuck that. No way."

"Jesus Christ!" Jericho took a breath made ragged by desire and frustration. "What happened to 'seize the day' and not being a dirty little secret and all the rest of that? You want to hear me say it? You were right, I was wrong, okay? Fuck everything else. Fuck everything that isn't you and me."

"Fuck Kayla?" Wade asked gently. "The shit with her dad is going to be a problem, for sure, but I think she's tough enough to get through it. If it comes out that on top of all that, her hand-picked under-sheriff is *also* in bed with criminals?" He didn't even bother to play with the double entendre. "You think her career could weather that? And what about yours? I know you're frustrated, but are you just going to walk away and leave Will rotting in jail when you think he's innocent? Are you going to ignore the fact that there's a killer out there, one who's going to get away with his crime if you and Kayla can't catch him?" He stepped a little closer, but there was nothing sexual in his movements, not anymore. "You going to do all that without hating yourself? Or hating me?"

"Something's gotta give. I can't keep—" Jericho didn't want to be a whiner. He wasn't the one in jail, he wasn't the one who loved her job and might lose it. Keith Wooderson wasn't going to kill *him* if justice wasn't done. What did he have to complain about, really?

But Wade's expression was calmer now. "You need some pressure release? Shit, Jay, we can do that. Only not here, where anyone might see us."

"It's more than pressure release," Jericho tried, but Wade didn't look convinced, and maybe it wasn't worth fighting about right then. "But if not here, then where? When?"

"Anytime you want," Wade said. "We could try tonight? At the old cabin, by the mine. Where we used to go. I can ditch the feds and hike through the trees; you can drive right up."

"That place was ratty fifteen years ago."

"You want us to fly to Paris instead?"

He absolutely did. Not Paris, necessarily, but somewhere else. Somewhere they could be themselves together, without all the extra bullshit. But that was a long-term dream. "I guess the cabin's okay for tonight. Yeah. Okay, I'll see you there."

The discussion seemed strangely practical, as if they were talking about something passionless and cold, but that impression changed when Jericho saw Wade's expression: Almost shy, almost tentative. Like he was hoping for happiness he knew better than to expect. It was fucking heartbreaking, especially since Jericho knew he'd given Wade every reason to be less than optimistic.

"Tonight," he repeated, and when he leaned in for a kiss, Wade didn't push him away. They kept it sweet, though, a promise rather than the start of anything.

"The feds are watching my phone," Wade said. "So if you can't make it, just . . . don't make it. If you aren't there, I'll know something came up. Don't contact me."

"I don't think I'm going to need to worry about that," Jericho said. Then he made himself step back, away from Wade. "Fifteen years," he said, mostly to himself. "A few more hours won't make that much of a difference."

He should have been right, and after he'd gone back to work he thought he *was* right. Poring over the case files Fernandez had brought with her, reviewing the evidence collected for the current case, looking for parallels or connections or points for further research—he did it all, more or less calmly, with only a general awareness of his evening's plans floating around in the back of his mind. That night he would see Wade, but until then, he was getting things done, and it was fine.

He took Fernandez over to review the crime scene, and they picked up dinner as they drove back, and everything was still fine. Sure, it was getting harder and harder to pay attention to the case, easier and easier to let his mind drift in directions that weren't exactly work appropriate, but that wasn't a big deal.

It was almost eight o'clock, and he was just packing up, thinking about stopping off at the drugstore on his way up the mountain to the old cabin, when he glanced out of his office and saw Wade slowly climbing the stairs. For half a second, Jericho let himself believe that there had just been a mix-up. Possibly they were supposed to be meeting at the station, or Wade had come by to give him a little more information from his mother, or ... something. Anything.

But after that half second, Jericho saw the FBI agents walking close behind Wade, saw the lawyer Wade always used trailing along after them, and knew that his plans for the evening had just changed. Wade was being brought in for questioning. Probably about Kayla's dad, but not necessarily. There were so many reasons the feds might want to talk to him.

Wade didn't even glance in Jericho's direction as he passed the office. No recognition, no acknowledgment. He was being discreet, of course, ignoring Jericho as a courtesy, not an insult. It was stupid to feel hurt by it.

Jericho sat in his office, alone, for far too long. He saw Fernandez leave for her motel and Kayla reluctantly drag herself home, probably to a night of worrying about her future and fuming about her father. He watched feds trail in and out of the interrogation room where Wade was being held. And, finally, he pushed away from his desk and went home. No stop at the drugstore, but after fifteen frustrating minutes of sitting on the couch, staring at the TV, he strode to the hall closet and yanked out his sleeping bag and a camping mattress. It wasn't like he was going to sleep properly at the apartment, so he might as well go up to the cabin and try to find some peace there. At least he'd be keeping his part of the bargain.

It was all strangely familiar, driving up the winding mountain road, then turning off onto a dirt track that would have been a lot smoother in an SUV instead of a Mustang. He and Wade used to camp out at the cabin pretty often when they were kids desperate for some privacy. Sneaking around had been fun then, but now it felt wrong.

And it was even more wrong to push open the creaky wooden door and step inside, flashlight illuminating a space that was too well-remembered, and too damn empty. Wade was supposed to be here, but he couldn't be. *Because of choices he made,* Jericho reminded himself. *Consequences for actions he's taken. Consequences you believe in.*

Unless, of course, he was being questioned not about information he'd received from Donald Morgan, but information he'd given. Information Jericho had asked him to give. Shit. Did Jericho believe in the consequences for that?

He played the flashlight over the cabin's interior, imagining for a moment that he was about to discover a stash of drugs or some other illicit item Wade would have arranged for him to find. A test or a dare or the first step in another bewildering manipulation. But the cabin was empty except for the same rickety wooden table and chairs that had been there decades ago, and a stained, mouse-nibbled mattress on the floor. The same one he and Wade had collapsed on so many times when they were kids? Quite possibly.

Jericho wrinkled his nose and unrolled his camping mattress in the middle of the floor, then shook his sleeping bag out on top of it. He'd slept worse places in his life, but he wasn't going near that old mattress, not willingly.

He kicked off his shoes and eased down so he was lying on his back, looking up at the roof. Might make more sense to go outside so he could see the stars, but he didn't move. Instead, he imagined he was somewhere else. A tropical island. Nothing too fancy, just a beach and some waves and a little hut with a clean mattress and nice sheets, an outdoor shower with fresh, cool water under the blazing sun—and Wade. Of course Wade would be there, adding to the perfection. He'd look at Jericho, and his eyes would glow with warmth that could so easily turn to heat. They'd touch each other, each as comfortable with the other's body as with his own. They'd lie in bed, the white sheets contrasting with their sun-darkened skin, and they'd talk, and laugh, and nobody would judge them or even notice them. It would just be Wade and Jericho, like it always should have been.

Somewhere in the middle of all that he faded into sleep, and when he woke to morning light puddling through the filthy, cracked window panes, he was still alone. He rolled to his feet and gathered up his makeshift bed, but instead of taking it out to the car with him, he left the sleeping bag and mattress tidily rolled on the table. Maybe it was stupid, but it felt like a gesture of hope, or at least of stubbornness. He wasn't giving up. Not again. Not yet.

CHAPTER 17

"Time to try for a search warrant?" Kayla asked after Jericho and Fernandez had run over the case with her. The bags under her eyes were more pronounced than usual and there were a few lines on her forehead Jericho hadn't noticed before, but she seemed focused on her work. "The problem is, we still haven't got much more than your instincts. I mean, it's *strange* for this guy to have been on the periphery of two cases that are so similar to each other, but I don't think that's going to be enough for a judge."

"And we'd be tipping him off," Jericho said. He'd come in to the office to find the interrogation room empty, but knew nothing else about what had happened with Wade the night before. Best to keep his mind on the case, especially since the feds wouldn't tell him anything even if he did ask. "Right now, Wooderson still thinks he got away with this, and that might be useful. Unless we think we're going to find something useful with a search warrant, I'm not sure there's a point to it."

"But if we don't do that, what else *do* we do?" Fernandez asked. She didn't appear any better rested than Kayla. What did it say that of the three of them, Jericho seemed to have had the best night's sleep, and he'd been lying on a hard floor in a rodent-infested cabin? Then again, he couldn't see himself—maybe he looked just as shitty as they did.

"How long do we keep Will locked up?" Jericho asked. "If we cut him loose, Wooderson's going to know something's going on, but I checked on him this morning and he seems pretty rough. The deputies are doing as much as they can to keep him calm, but he's locked up, he's fucked up from whatever he saw—we need to start making things better for him, soon."

Kayla sighed as if the air was being pushed out of her body by a great weight. "One thing we have to do—and I know you aren't going to like it, Jay, and I can't say I like it much myself—we need to talk to the FBI. If we are dealing with a serial killer—an interstate serial killer—that's their gig. Unless they order us off, we can keep investigating the local case, and, Detective Fernandez, you can keep investigating things in Akron. But looking for links between the two? That's FBI territory."

Jericho knew she was right, and a part of him welcomed the idea of making all this someone else's problem. He was a small-town under-sheriff, and even when he'd been in LA working homicide, he'd never dealt with a serial killer. It was a totally different mind-set, and he only had training, not experience, to help him understand it. He didn't *want* to understand it. So why not let go?

"Will they take it seriously?" he asked. "Like you said, it's almost all instinct right now, not much real evidence."

"I think they'll consider it, yeah. We have to give them the chance."

"And Will? Can we cut him loose while they're looking at it?"

Kayla made a face. "That's the prosecutor's call. I'll update her, see what she wants to do. I imagine it'll mostly depend on the FBI response."

"Okay." Jericho turned to Fernandez. "You okay with that? Have you got a next step in mind for yourself?"

"I want to reexamine the brother's death," she said, "and do some more digging into the background there. See what's going on in this fucker's brain."

Kayla spoke carefully. "Is your department going to support you in that investigation?"

"My department wants me to shut up and let it go. It's a closed case, after all." Fernandez looked at Kayla, then turned to Jericho. "But some cases, you *can't* let go. The case won't let *you* go. This one?" She shook her head. "It doesn't matter what my department wants. I'm on this case until Keith Wooderson goes down, or until I do. So, yeah, you need to bring the feds in. I get it, and if they take it seriously, that's great. They know about this shit. But if they don't take it seriously? That's not going to even slow me down. I've got interviews set up back in Ohio, reviewing Wooderson's past using the new focus we've got on this case, but if you need me up here for anything, you give me a call and I'm here."

"Okay," Kayla said. "We haven't got a lot of financial resources to offer, but we're definitely interested in sharing information. And unless you object, I'll get in touch with your department and let them know we're reviewing the case up here and are planning to involve the FBI."

"Can't hurt," Fernandez said. "Thanks."

And that was that. Jericho and Fernandez spent some more time going over their respective cases, making sure they hadn't missed anything, and then Fernandez left for the airport. Jericho stared at the files on his desk for a few minutes before he pushed to his feet. He was going on patrol. Community policing, being a visible presence, observing and understanding—he didn't care what jargon he could use as an excuse. He was restless, and he didn't want to stare at paper anymore.

His drive started fairly responsibly with a tour through the rough areas on the edges of the town. There were a lot of people out there who would do well to be reminded that there was law enforcement keeping an eye on things, and he needed to maintain his feel for the streets.

It was harder to justify his decision to cruise down Main Street, slowing outside Scotty Hawk's garage before coming to his senses and driving on. He was on the clock, in uniform, driving a damn squad car. It was *not* the time for acting like a teenager scoping out his crush.

But when he got to the hardware store, he didn't hesitate before pulling into a parking spot and heading for the door. Didn't hesitate at all, not until he saw the man standing in the doorway.

"Mr. Wooderson," he said, keeping his voice as level as he could. *Be cool, don't blow it, don't lose the war because you want to win a battle.* "How are your daughters? Not still shaken up, I hope?"

"They're recovering." Wooderson smiled calmly, but there was an unfamiliar intensity to his voice as he added, "I heard you went by the school, asking about them. Or were you asking about *me*?"

Jericho should have been chagrined. Hell, he should have been something stronger than that. He hadn't pushed Mrs. Andarov for confidentiality because he'd thought it would make her *more* likely to spread the word. And now his actions had come back to bite him in the ass. Wooderson knew Jericho had been looking into him, and the bastard probably had at least some idea of what had been discovered. It was a serious problem for the case. But instead of being upset, Jericho felt a strange sense of glee. Enough sneaking around and setting up strategies. It was time for the endgame to begin.

"I like to know who I'm dealing with," Jericho said calmly. "You're new to town, and I was hoping to get a bit of background. I hope you don't mind?" *You don't have anything to hide, do you, asshole?*

"No," Wooderson said with a seemingly genuine smile. "I don't mind at all. I'm very pleased, really." He peered into the hardware store, then back at Jericho. "It's much nicer in there, now, don't you think? Without that animal roaming around, dirtying the place up? Animals shouldn't live with humans."

"When you say animal, you mean Will?" *You* are *that much of an asshole?* "You thought he interfered with your hardware shopping experience? That must have been really, really terrible for you."

"But not anymore," Wooderson said. He was breathing strangely, as if he'd been walking too fast and was just a little out of breath. "Now, it's fine."

"Wow. Lucky. Or maybe not just luck?" This was the dynamic Fernandez had described. Wooderson *did* want to share, want to gloat, want to make law enforcement know he'd beaten them and was out of reach. It was part of the thrill, part of his motivation.

"I don't believe in luck," Wooderson said. "I believe in creating opportunities, and then following through with bold action."

"Is that right? Can you give me an example of how that might happen? Like, in this case. You didn't like having an animal messing up your hardware store, so . . . you created an opportunity?"

Wooderson's smile was patronizing. Jericho's silly games were beneath him. "Sometimes I don't need to do anything. Sometimes the Lord provides."

"Oh, the Lord's getting involved, now? Not luck. So, can you clarify for me? How did the Lord provide in this case?"

"I'm not saying He did, Mr. Crewe. I'm just saying He *sometimes* does."

And now Jericho saw what might be his chance. Fernandez had been a woman, and someone like Wooderson? Someone who killed female prostitutes for convenience? He'd react differently to female authority than he would to male authority. He'd have reacted one way to Fernandez, a totally different way to Jericho now. So Jericho made himself smirk.

"Sounds like you're not saying anything at all," he said. "Lots of noise, but not any actual content." Then he shrugged, trying to make his broad shoulders even wider, trying to project whatever dismissive macho vibe would be most enraging to a man like Wooderson. "Let me know when you've got the balls to actually say something." And he headed for the hardware store door, deliberately stepping into Wooderson's space a little as he moved.

"The *balls*?" Wooderson squeaked as Jericho pulled the door open. "You think I don't have the balls?"

Jericho looked over his shoulder. "Maybe they haven't dropped yet?" he suggested, and let the door swing shut behind him.

He kept his pace steady as he strolled up the aisle to the counter, but his heart was racing, adrenaline pumping through his veins. The man was a killer, a murderer, and he wanted to confess. He wanted Jericho to know what he'd done. Maybe he *needed* it. How hard could he be pushed?

"Jericho," Mr. Appleby said from an aisle near the counter. "What can I get for you?"

"Nothing, thanks." He tried to keep at least the surface of his attention focused on the conversation. "I just wanted to check in. You've been going to visit Will, right? How does he seem, to you?"

Mr. Appleby's face was impassive. "He seems very, very upset, Jericho. How would you expect him to feel?"

Well, okay, that was a fair answer to a stupid question. Why the hell had he come here? What had he intended, before he was distracted by the murdering bastard in the doorway? "I'd expect him to feel that way," he tried. "But we're hoping—I'm hoping—to get him out of there pretty soon." And in order for that to happen, Jericho needed to prove to the county attorney that Will wasn't a reasonable suspect. He cast his eyes around the store. "You don't sell any sort of electronic stuff, do you? Recording equipment? Microphones, micro-recorders—anything at all micro?"

"We have a couple micro*waves* in the housewares department," Mr. Appleby said. "But I don't think you could count on them to record much."

"No, probably not." Jericho stepped into an aisle, far enough that he was shielded from view of the street, and pulled out his cell phone. It had a voice recorder, but not a great one. It was something, though. If he could get Wooderson riled enough to spill anything useful, there'd be a record of it.

He tried to find a view of the street, but it was blocked by the center barrier of the aisle, a display of flashlights, lanterns, and radios on his side of the display. Mr. Appleby, however, was standing by the counter, out in the open.

"Sir," Jericho said. "Would it be possible for you to be very casual about something? It needs to not seem obvious. Do you understand what I'm saying?"

"If you're about to ask me to check if that asshole Keith Wooderson is still lurking around in my doorway? Then, yes, I understand completely, and, yes, he is. The bastard's been in here every day, sometimes twice a day, ever since Will was arrested."

"Does he buy anything?"

"Small items, sometimes. But mostly? Mostly, I'd swear he was here for the suffering. He wants to talk about Will to me, to Mary, to anyone who'll listen. And the things he says are far from kind."

"Do you remember him coming in before Will was arrested?" *Do you remember him buying a two-by-four and some grass seed? He'd have paid cash so we'd trace it back to Will's workplace, but without a paper trail leading to the real killer.*

"I don't recall that, no. He may have, of course. But I don't remember it."

"Yeah—just a long shot." Jericho made sure the recording function on his phone was turned on. "Do you think you could watch what's about to happen outside? It'll probably be nothing, but just in case, could you jot down what's going on, as you see it happening?"

"Jot it down?" Mr. Appleby asked. Then he pulled out his own phone. "Or film it?"

"Well, yeah, that would be much better." Good reminder to not assume the elderly were completely unable to handle modern technology. "Okay, is it recording now?"

Mr. Appleby tapped the screen a few times, then nodded. "All systems go."

"Try to be as discreet as you can. But if I do my job right, he won't be looking in here, anyway."

Jericho started for the door, but Mr. Appleby's voice stopped him halfway. "Jericho? Is this about Will? Whatever you're doing, is it part of helping Will?"

"It's about catching a serial killer, Mr. Appleby." It felt good to know the words were being recorded by two separate devices, as if that somehow gave them the gravitas they otherwise lacked. "And, yes, if we can do that, it will help Will. Absolutely."

"Okay, then," Mr. Appleby said, and as Jericho glanced back he saw the old man angling himself behind a display of flower seeds, setting up a clear sight line that wouldn't be obvious from outside the store.

"Thank you," Jericho said, and he took the last steps toward the door.

For a moment, it seemed as if Wooderson had left, and Jericho cursed himself. He'd had his chance, and he'd blown it. He was a soldier, a grunt, not a fucking intel officer. Not a spy. He should have stayed a beat cop because he couldn't cut it as a real detective. He was out of his league, and he shouldn't have fooled himself into thinking otherwise.

Then Wooderson stepped out of the doorway just down the street, his gaze fixed on Jericho.

"What were you saying about me not having any balls?" the man demanded.

For a beautiful, glorious moment, Jericho thought Wooderson might pull a gun. It would be so simple if he did. Jericho was a fast draw and a good shot. If Wooderson's hand moved, if it went out of sight, Jericho would pull and aim, and if he saw the glint of metal, he'd fire and this would all be over. Fernandez's case would be closed for real, no one else would get hurt, and Jericho would find enough evidence, one way or another, to get Will out of trouble. It would all be so much easier.

But the bastard didn't go along with Jericho's plan. He just stalked forward, eyes too bright, too fixed, too focused on Jericho's face. "What were you saying?" he demanded again, his voice shriller with every word.

"To you?" Jericho said. "I don't think I was saying anything to you. Why would I bother?"

"You're trying to wind me up," Wooderson said. "Trying to get me to say something I shouldn't."

So the guy wasn't completely clueless. But Jericho channeled his best Wade-Granger disdain and said, "Yeah, that's it exactly. So you should shut the fuck up—that'd really teach me a lesson."

Wooderson's face turned red, and he leaned forward, his stare ferocious. Strangely, the aggressiveness made Jericho feel safer; if this bastard had a weapon, he'd have already drawn it, and there was no way he'd be a threat hand-to-hand.

"You don't know who you're dealing with," Wooderson hissed.

"Sure, tough guy." Jericho leaned nonchalantly against the hardware store window. "So go for it. Tell me who I'm dealing with. Impress me."

For a moment, Jericho truly believed it was going to work. Wooderson's snarl, his tense body, his wild eyes, they all spoke of someone on the edge of control. Jericho snorted dismissively, then waited for the explosion.

But Wooderson pulled himself back. "I don't need to prove myself to you."

"Why do you hate them?" Jericho asked. "People like Will. What's the issue there? Is it just that you have to think you're better than *someone*, and you're so pathetic yourself that you need to find a person who's really struggling in order to compete? Or is it something else? Maybe your brother. Did your brother touch you in a bad place, Keith? Are you angry at him and taking it out on people like him?"

"You have no idea what you're talking about."

"Yeah, I do. You kill prostitutes because they're easy victims, you frame disabled people because they're easy victims—you're fucking weak. Pathetic."

Wooderson's smile showed too many teeth to be a gesture of goodwill. "If you had a single drop of evidence for any of that, we'd be having this conversation at the police station, not on the sidewalk."

"We'll see you at the station soon enough," Jericho said. "Enjoy your last little bit of freedom. And know that you failed, this time. Will isn't going to be punished for this; we're working on cutting him loose right now. It's clear he didn't hurt Lorraine. You went to a lot of trouble for nothing."

"I don't know what you're talking about." Wooderson's body was more relaxed now—the opportunity was gone. "But, certainly, if you'd like to discuss it further, you can contact my lawyer. We'll see how he feels about your threats."

And with that, he turned and strode jauntily along the sidewalk. He'd been shaken for a moment, but that was all.

Jericho, on the other hand, felt as if he'd been kicked in the gut. Wooderson was right: there was no evidence. For all his certainty, Jericho had no damn proof of the man's involvement, and no real idea of how to *get* any proof.

Maybe the FBI would do better, but he wasn't sure there was even enough evidence to convince them to look into the case. Or if they did, they'd take their time, adding it to a long list of cases to be investigated when they had space in their schedule.

That was when Jericho stopped worrying about justice for Lorraine and Will. It wasn't that he didn't think they deserved it, but standing there on the sidewalk, watching Wooderson practically strut down the street away from him, he realized that they couldn't be the priority anymore. Instead, he, like Angela Fernandez, had to worry about the *next* people Wooderson would target. The bastard had skipped out of Akron when Fernandez caught on to him, and she hadn't been able to track him. He'd known enough to stay off the grid: hadn't updated his license at the DMV, hadn't told the kids' school where he was going, hadn't left a forwarding address for his mail, or changed his address with anyone. He'd just dropped off the planet.

He could do it again. He *would* do it again. And Jericho would watch for reports of prostitutes apparently murdered by intellectually disabled men and get in touch with the investigators when he saw a similar case. That would help the men, maybe, would shorten their time as suspects, but it wouldn't protect the women. It wasn't good enough to wait for the next time; Jericho needed to *prevent* the next time.

He went back inside the store and arranged for Mr. Appleby to email him the video from his phone; it wouldn't be much use, but it could be added to the case file, at least, along with Jericho's audio recording. Maybe the combination would be enough to convince the FBI that Wooderson was unbalanced. Maybe.

Then he climbed into his cruiser and called Kay. "He knows we're on to him," he said after explaining what had happened. "There's no point being subtle anymore."

"And subtlety's never been your strong suit, after all."

"I didn't make this happen, Kay. I wasn't trying to blow the case open, I promise. The school tipped him off, and he just knew."

"I know," she said. "But this was not the plan. It's more cowboy bullshit, whether you meant for it to happen or not. I've made calls to the FBI, and I'm waiting for someone to get back to me. I'd rather not drag the ones in our office into it, since they're not the right division, but maybe I'll talk to them and see if they can hurry their colleagues up."

She was talking about asking for a favor from the men who were prosecuting her father and investigating her. But Jericho couldn't think of a better option.

"Let me know if I can do anything," he said, and they ended the call.

He sat in the cruiser, fighting temptation, then gave in and hit dial on the number he'd been wanting to call all morning.

"Under-sheriff," Wade answered.

"Hey. You okay?"

"Is this a courtesy call? A new service offered by the department for those who have recently enjoyed their hospitality?"

He was trying to cover, Jericho realized. Trying to remind him that the feds were listening, and Jericho needed to be acting like the cop he was.

But he'd meant it when he said he didn't care anymore. "Can you meet me? I want to talk to you."

"Not a good idea, Officer. I don't have anything to add to the thorough statement I gave to the FBI last night."

"Did you recite the alphabet for them? I hear they like that."

Finally, there was a little inflection in Wade's voice. "This isn't a joke, Jericho. You know better."

"I don't care what I know."

"Well, I do. Don't call me again."

The line went dead, leaving Jericho staring at the phone in his hand. What had just happened? How much of it had been real, how much a performance for the listening feds?

All of it had been for the feds. It had to be fake. Whatever he and Wade were doing, it had the weight of inevitability behind it. Neither of them had a choice; neither of them could simply walk away. It had to be affecting both of them, because if it was just Jericho? If Wade wasn't coping with this desperate, irrational need? No, Jericho wouldn't even waste time thinking about what that might mean.

He pulled the cruiser out into traffic, back to his aimless driving. There were no new leads to pursue, nothing useful to do. He was relying on the FBI to deal with Wooderson, expecting Kayla to deal with her father's issues, and now Wade, the one part of his life that had actually seemed to be moving in a positive direction, was shutting him down. He was just done with it, all of it.

Probably he needed another hard workout and should go back to the station gym, but instead he found himself driving up into the mountains. As he drove, as the trees surrounded him, he calmed down. Wade had been talking to the feds, not to Jericho. It was clear. It was fine.

By the time he reached the cabin, he wasn't even a little surprised to see the beat-up truck parked beside it. Not Wade's usual vehicle, but that made sense if he was having to sneak away from federal surveillance in order to keep things as secret as he had clearly decided they should be.

The cabin door was open, and as Jericho pulled up, the inner shadows solidified and became Wade's lean body as the man stepped outside and shook his head in his trademark amused dismay. "Was there some part of 'don't use the phone' you found difficult to understand?" he called as Jericho climbed out of the cruiser.

"Is there some part of 'I don't care what people know' that *you* find difficult to understand?"

"You're fucking impulsive, young Crewe." Wade moved closer, his expression warm and relaxed. "A week ago you wanted this all to be secret, now you want to advertise it to the world. But you need to remember—once the world knows, you can't switch back again when you change your mind. Once the cat's out of the bag, you're not going to be able to cram it back in."

"That's something for me to worry about, not you."

"Well, when you *were* worrying about it, that was true. But now that you've stopped, seems like I need to come in and take over."

Jericho was suddenly exhausted. The adrenaline was leaving his system now that he was somewhere he felt safe. With some*one* who made him feel safe. "Can we, I don't know, can we talk about that another time? Right now I just—"

"Okay," Wade said as he stepped forward, calm and steady. He wrapped a hand around the back of Jericho's neck. "We'll talk about it later. For now?" His kiss was gentle. An invitation, but a nonspecific one. It was clear enough: comfort, competition, anger, or passion; if Jericho needed it, Wade was offering to provide it.

Jericho deepened the kiss. He needed all of it. Everything Wade had, Jericho wanted. He let himself be shuffled backward, guided around the rough terrain until his back was against a wide tree trunk. "You're good, Jay," Wade murmured, his lips moving against Jericho's jaw, then his neck. "Everything's good. It's only you and me, okay?"

It was lucky there was a tree to lean against, or Jericho might have slumped right to the ground. Everything was so much more than good, so much more than okay. "You're perfect, Wade," he managed, and felt Wade's lips curve in response.

"Well, that's just your boner talking." Wade dragged his hand across the strained polyester of Jericho's uniform pants. "And your dick has never been known for its good judgment."

"It knows what it likes," Jericho responded.

"And you're okay? Whatever had you worked up, you're over it?"

"Over it?" Jericho said. "Keith Wooderson knows we're after him, and I expect he's going to try to book it out of here before we can build enough of a case to even charge him. So he's going to find another town, another hooker, and—" Jericho shook his head so violently Wade pulled away. "And there's nothing I can do about it. So, fuck, I don't know. I need to forget about it. Just one more way the world is broken, right? Is that what you'd say?"

"Sounds like I don't need to say it, not when you can say it for yourself." Wade kissed the corner of Jericho's mouth. "You want me to help you forget about all that? That why you're here?"

"That's part of it."

Wade didn't push for the rest. He just tugged at Jericho's tie, loosening it and then pulling it free. "Okay, then. Let's get rid of some clothes."

It had been quite a while since Jericho had been naked outdoors. He'd forgotten how much more intense everything felt—the sun's warmth, the tree trunk's rough bark, the cool whisper of the breeze—when there was no clothing to diminish the impact. Wade's mouth left a damp trail on Jericho's belly, and the wind blew across and gave him a trail of goose bumps, showing where Wade had been.

Jericho threw his head back and let himself get lost in the sensations. He felt taken care of, protected, encouraged. He explored Wade's body, one that he had once known as well as he knew his own, and rediscovered its beauty. When Wade reached for his pile of clothes and retrieved a foil package and a little bottle, it was inevitable and completely natural. Wade rolled the condom onto Jericho's cock while kissing him, then turned around and looked back over his shoulder in an exaggerated, almost coquettish way that made Jericho smile. Wade, the source of every temptation.

And for a while, there in the forest, with no one to watch or judge them, Jericho was more than happy to give in to that temptation. It was Wade, and it was Jericho, and they were together—all was right with the world.

CHAPTER 18

It was a harsh transition to drive down from the mountain a couple of hours later, back into the tumult of the town. By the time Jericho arrived at the sheriff's station, Kayla had already had her meeting with the feds, and she shook her head when Jericho asked her about it.

"They listened," she said. "They're going to investigate."

"But they're not putting a rush on it," he finished for her. "They're not treating it as a priority."

"They're gathering information, they're going to talk to some experts back East, look at the two cases, try to sort something out."

"He knows we're on to him. He's disappeared before."

"What do you want me to say? What do you want *them* to say, or to do? They can't arrest him with no evidence any more than we can."

"Goddamn it," Jericho said, mostly to the ceiling. All the peace and relaxation he'd found with Wade had drained right out of him, and he was back to being tense and frustrated. "So what are we going to do?"

"We'll keep working the case. Keep trying to find evidence. Now that he knows we're on to him, we can talk to his neighbors, bring him in for questioning and try to shake whatever alibi he's got cooked up. I don't think we've got enough for a search warrant, but I'll talk to the prosecutor about it, see what she says."

"And Will? You'll talk to her about getting Will out?"

"I'll talk to her," Kayla said. "But, shit, Jay, he's still our best suspect. He's the only one we've got any damn evidence against."

"I'm going to get him a better lawyer. Someone with more experience, more fire."

"*You're* going to do that," she said. "You mean you're going to pay for it? Yourself?"

"Yeah. I guess so."

She gave him a long look, then said, "Be smart about it. Talk to Ned Appleby and see if he'll be your beard. Hell, see if he'll go further than that. He was trying to raise money for Will's bail, so see if he'll try to raise money for this, instead. You can chip in whatever you need to, but get the Applebys and anyone else who believes in Will to give a little too. This town takes care of its own, you know, and if they believe he's innocent, they'll step up. But they need to do it with the Applebys in charge, not you. Okay?"

"Yeah, okay," Jericho agreed. No point in making things more difficult for Kayla than they had to be, and an under-sheriff publicly supporting the defense in a sheriff's department case would definitely not help appearances. "I'll talk to him."

He stood up and was halfway to the door of her office when she said, "Jay?"

He turned to see her burrowing through the purse she stashed in her desk drawer while she was on the job.

"Here." She pulled all the bills out of her wallet. "And let me know if I can help any other way."

"You sure? Might come a time when you'd like to honestly say you weren't involved in this."

"Might come a time when I'd like to honestly say I was," she returned, and stretched the bills a little farther toward him. "Either way—at least I'll know I did what I thought was right."

It was probably unnecessarily saccharine, but he said it anyway. "You're a good sheriff, Kay. Doing what you think is right? That's how the person in this job *should* be making their decisions. They shouldn't be worried about politics or people-pleasing or whatever else Jackson is always up to. You know that, don't you?"

"I think I'm good at the job, or I wouldn't be doing it. But what the people think?" She shrugged. "We'll have to wait and see, I guess."

"I'd really like to punch your dad in the face."

"You've wanted to punch him in the face since you were fourteen years old. Don't go digging for an excuse, Crewe."

"You're okay, though? I mean—" What the hell *did* he mean? "You want to get a drink sometime and bitch about shit, let me know."

She nodded, and he let it go.

It took about ten minutes to drive down to the hardware store and talk to Mr. Appleby, who responded with the enthusiasm Jericho would have predicted. The man was the kind of Christian who Christ probably would have actually liked.

After that he went out to the highway and pulled over a couple of speeding cars with out-of-state license plates, just so he could feel like he'd done something vaguely constructive with his time. Of course he should get in touch with Fernandez and let her know how the case had changed, but he couldn't bring himself to do it. She cared too much, and it would hit her hard when she found out things had gotten screwed up again.

But that way of thinking was too damn passive. Things hadn't just gotten screwed up, Jericho had screwed them up. He could find excuses for himself—he hadn't known what he was digging into at the start, so there'd been no reason to be stealthy about how he got his information—but that wasn't good enough. He'd found Wooderson sufficiently strange to be worth investigating, so he should have made sure everyone knew his questions were confidential. Mrs. Andarov was a busybody, but she wasn't a psychopath; if he'd tried, he probably could have persuaded her to keep her mouth shut at least for a while

As it was, he'd tipped off a murderer because he'd been too damn casual in his investigation. Whatever Wooderson did after this, whoever he killed next, that woman's blood would be on Jericho's hands.

Just like Lorraine's already was. Jericho had sworn an oath to serve and protect, but his department hadn't protected her. They'd pushed her into working in a more dangerous environment, they'd treated her like a nuisance, a problem to be solved instead of a human being to be helped.

He'd been a wild kid in this town and been so resentful of the way people judged him, and he'd grown up to be just the kind of hypocrite he'd despised. He was the kind of cop who made people like Lorraine, people like Sandi Granger, hate and distrust cops.

But he didn't have to be that kind of cop forever. He could start making things better instead of maintaining the status quo.

So he needed to find something, enough to hold Wooderson while the feds figured things out. He sat there on the side of the highway, barely noticing the cars that slammed on their brakes as soon as they saw the cruiser, and tried to track his way through it all.

If Will could talk, maybe he could shed some light on things. If Lorraine could talk, maybe she'd have something to say. But as it was, Jericho was on his own.

The lab reports from the crime scene were taking forever to process. Maybe they'd come up with something, although it was hard to know what it would be. Lorraine worked out of her home, so there was a clear excuse if Wooderson's DNA or fingerprints turned up at the scene. Lorraine's appointment book might have been useful, but it was still missing.

Which meant it probably *did* have incriminating details. Otherwise, Wooderson would have planted it somewhere to be found with Will's name in it.

But it was pretty damn easy to get rid of an item made of paper. A good fire, with carefully stirred ashes that were then sent to the dump? If Wooderson had wanted the book gone, it was gone.

Jericho sat there until the sun began to set behind the mountains, tracing over every aspect of the case, searching for the glitch, the opportunity. Then he put the car into gear and headed back into town. He knew what he should do. Get something to eat, go to the apartment, maybe go for a run, and then get a good night's sleep. That was what a responsible adult would do.

Instead, he pointed the car toward the houses on the edge of town, just a few blocks away from Lorraine's place. He parked across the street from the modest bungalow where Wooderson and his daughters lived, and he waited.

It was almost dark when the front door opened and Wooderson appeared. He was carrying a cardboard box, and he brought it down and set it in the trunk of the car.

The bastard was just going on about his life. No fear, no anger, just doing some chores. Maybe already thinking of the next woman he'd kill.

Jericho's throat was tight when he swallowed, and his hands had turned into fists.

He'd never planted evidence before, but . . . maybe this was the time. If it had ever been justified, it was justified now.

No. Too damn risky. He didn't know what he was doing, and if he got caught, it could jeopardize the entire case.

He was searching his mind for another strategy when Wooderson came back out with another box, and then a duffel bag and a knapsack.

Jesus Christ.

Jericho stared across the street. The man was packing up. He was leaving town. Were his daughters still inside, waiting?

No, he'll leave them behind. They're how he was traced this time. He won't take the chance of the same thing happening again. Oh god. It's all going to happen again.

Jericho was out of the car and crossing the street before he'd knew it. He had no plan, no goal, but he was moving anyway. *Fucking typical. Just charge in and hope for the best.* Kayla wouldn't be impressed.

But this wasn't about Kayla. Kayla followed the book, and that was right for her. But Jericho? Was it right for him?

As Wooderson locked his front door, Jericho moved to stand by the driver's door of the car, and when Wooderson turned, he saw Jericho and froze. There was only a moment of surprise, or maybe alarm, but enough to be sweet. Unfortunately, Wooderson's smirk quickly returned, and Jericho realized his own presence was going to make this even more enjoyable for the sick son of a bitch.

"Deputy Crewe! You've come to see me off?" Wooderson swaggered down the walkway toward the car. "That's very kind. I hope the police in the next place I live are just as pleasant. And just as easy to work with."

"So you're leaving?" Jericho needed a plan. He needed to *do* something. "What about your girls? They not going with you?"

"Not this time." Wooderson sounded mildly regretful, like he was leaving behind a favorite plant. "Youngsters need stability, and with my lifestyle—my diverse interests—I think they'll be happier with someone less footloose."

"Where are they? You can't just leave them."

"They're with friends. And I've sent a message to some people who can reach my ex-wife. She'll take care of them. Little angels, they are. Anyone would be glad to have them."

Well, that was something. When the ex arrived, Jericho could talk to her, could talk to the girls. But there was no real reason to believe he'd learn anything new, and even if he did, no reason to believe he'd be able to act on it, not with Wooderson already vanished.

"Where you headed?" Jericho asked.

Wooderson laughed. "I'm not sure. I've been thinking of selling the car—they can be such anchors, you know? I could rely on public transit to get me anywhere I need to go."

With no car, it was that much harder to trace someone. A middle-aged, middle-sized white guy with a bland, nondescript face—it would be practically impossible to find him with no kids and no car. He could start a new email address and a new PayPal account, find new clients, and be gone.

"You're going to kill again," Jericho said. He was talking to himself as much as to Wooderson. "If I don't stop you, someone else is going to die. Maybe more than one person, if they aren't quick enough to catch you at the next stop."

Wooderson's smile was placid, almost beatific. "You can't stop me, Deputy. You have absolutely no evidence. No possible excuse for arresting me."

Jericho didn't need an excuse; he could just do it. He could arrest the bastard, hold him for as long as possible, and hope that gave the FBI and the rest of the team time to find the evidence they needed. But there wouldn't be much opportunity. Even if Jericho lied and said Wooderson had attacked him, he'd be free on bail in no time, or released without charges.

Wooderson stepped forward. "So, out of my way, Deputy. I've got an appointment in—well, I'm not quite sure where, yet. But I'm eager to find out."

His smile faded a little when Jericho didn't move, and a little more when he saw Jericho's hand resting on his gun. He shook his head. "No. You don't have the guts."

"Guts? You think it takes *guts* to do what you do?" There was an unfamiliar trembling in Jericho's voice, but he kept talking anyway.

"You think it takes guts to shoot an unarmed person? That's a sign of courage to you?"

"I've never *shot* anyone, Deputy. Now, step away from my car."

Jericho drew his gun. His mind was in turmoil, hopping around too quickly for him to be able to think anything through. Was there another way? Was this right? Was there any way he could do it and not get caught? Was he willing to throw his whole life away for this? His job, sure. But his freedom? He'd be in jail for a long time, or else he'd become a fugitive, scuttling around forever, never able to stay anywhere or build anything. He'd lose Wade. Whatever was going on with Wade, he'd lose it.

But what would happen if he *didn't* stop Wooderson? He thought of Fernandez, flying across the country on her own time, her own dime, obsessed with the man she'd let get away. He thought of Nikki and the kids, getting beat up because Jericho hadn't stopped Eli. He'd have blood on his hands if he did this, but he'd have someone else's blood, some innocent woman's blood on his hands, if he didn't.

He raised the gun, and Wooderson's eyes widened. "You—" he started, and then his head jerked back, the black hole in his forehead seeming to grow as his body tumbled to the ground.

The *bang* came a moment later, and Jericho stared down at the gun he was still pointing toward where Wooderson had been standing.

Wooderson was dead, the pool of blood by his head spreading gradually, a dark gloss on the driveway.

But Jericho hadn't pulled the trigger. And the sound—the delay—someone else had fired, someone at a distance.

Jericho whirled to look at the darkened street. There was a car already driving away from down the block, red taillights the only thing visible. The car had been closer when the shot was fired, close enough that there would have been a clear line of sight. The shooter was in the car, and was leaving the scene.

Jericho stayed where he was for a moment, then bent over and checked Wooderson's neck for a pulse. There was none, just as he'd known there wouldn't be.

He straightened in time to see the taillights disappear as the car turned a corner. Then he walked slowly back to his cruiser. Wooderson was dead, and Jericho hadn't killed him. And he wasn't going to chase after the person who had.

CHAPTER 19

It was a long night of answering questions and being treated with a significant level of suspicion, but Jericho didn't mind. Wooderson was dead. No more desperate women were going to die, no more vulnerable men were going to suffer needlessly. And Jericho's story would hold up, since it was almost all true. He hadn't mentioned that he'd drawn his gun, and didn't think he'd be caught out in that; the initial survey had found a neighbor who'd seen Jericho sitting in the cruiser and then standing and crossing the road, but the corner of his own house had blocked his view of what had happened in the Wooderson driveway. So the neighbor's testimony, combined with clear evidence that the shot had been fired from a rifle some distance away, made it obvious that Jericho was a witness, not a shooter.

Still, it was almost dawn by the time he left the station. He needed to go home and get some sleep, but instead, he found himself heading for the mountains.

There was an altogether different battered pickup parked in front of the old cabin, and Jericho very carefully did not examine the taillights to see if their shape was familiar. Instead, he pushed the door gently open and stepped inside to find Wade lying on his back on the camping mattress and sleeping bag, eyes closed.

Jericho shut the door behind himself and undid his utility belt.

"You okay?" Wade asked from the floor. He sat up, slow and graceful, and pointed to a bottle on the rickety table. "Need a drink?"

"You taking care of me?" There was a definite instinct to keep his mouth shut and not push to hear answers he might not want, but Jericho overrode it. He needed to know. "Like you looked after me earlier tonight?"

Wade sighed and stretched over until he could reach the bottle himself. He spun the lid off with one practiced move of his thumb, lifted it to his lips, took a mouthful, and extend the bottle in Jericho's direction.

Jericho took it—no reason not to—and as he swallowed, as the familiar warm bite hit his throat, he was glad of it. He lowered himself gingerly onto one of the wooden chairs, cautious until he was sure it would take his weight, then leaned forward so his head was only a little higher than Wade's. He handed the bottle back, and then he waited.

Finally Wade said, "I'll always try to look after you, Jay. You know that."

"By sacrificing yourself?"

Wade's shrug was just a dance of shadows. "If I had to, yeah. But in this case? This case that we're not going to talk about in detail, for everyone's sake? Not much risk. Not much sacrifice. Remember what you said when you asked me to talk to Kay's dad? I know how to do these things without getting caught."

Of course he did. The ballistics wouldn't be traceable to him, and if he were brought in, he'd have an easily reinforced story of hunting or target shooting to explain any gunfire residue on his clothes or his vehicle. He'd have driven one of Scotty Hawk's many half-wrecked trucks, one that didn't have any trackers on it, one that the feds wouldn't recognize. He'd probably shaken his surveillance off by trekking through the woods to another car. He'd have done it smart. He'd taken a human life, and he wouldn't be punished for it. Suspected? Maybe, if anyone ever decided he had a motive. But he was used to living under suspicion.

"You were sure it had to be done?" Jericho asked.

"*You* were sure," Wade replied calmly, and he lifted the bottle. "You were ready to do it yourself, but you knew it wasn't smart. So I took care of it for you."

He took care of it. Killing another human being was taking care of something.

Jericho wasn't squeamish about killing; he'd seen enough of it in the military, and done enough of it himself. But that had been different. He'd never known one of the people he or his friends killed.

Wooderson had been sick and dangerous, but he'd been a civilian. A father. One of the people Jericho had sworn to serve and protect.

And Wade had confirmed that he'd killed Wooderson because of *Jericho's* decision. The legal responsibility might have been shifted, but the moral weight was harder to move.

"You okay?" Wade asked, just as he had when Jericho first came in. Apparently he still wanted to hear an answer.

But Jericho didn't have the words to express how he was. "Why'd you send me after Cory Barker?" he asked. "What was that for?"

"He was cooking meth in a residential neighborhood. I assumed you'd want to take care of that before somebody got hurt."

"What else?" Jericho knew Wade was watching him closely, trying to figure out his mood. So that was two of them who weren't exactly clear how Jericho was supposed to feel about any of this.

After a long wait, Wade shrugged. "I heard you were looking for snakes."

Too long of a wait for an answer that shitty. Jericho pushed to his feet and took a half step toward the door.

Wade snorted like he was going to call Jericho's bluff, going to let him leave and head out into the night alone. But then his expression softened a little. "I honestly don't know, Jay. It just . . . occurred to me. I don't run meth, so it wasn't a business thing. I know him, and he's an asshole, but so are lots of other people in town, and I'm not planning ways to get any of *them* busted. Or at least not *all* of them. This was just—it was an idea I had. I didn't see a downside, so I let it happen."

"Let it happen or made it happen?"

"Let. I wasn't going to push it. I didn't have a backup plan." He was quiet for a moment. "Remember when we were kids? Playing in the stream behind your place? Building dams and barriers and whatever, seeing which way the water would go? Sometimes you could drop one stone in just the right place and the whole stream would change course. Remember that?" Wade waited for agreement, but continued without it. "I told Elijah about the snakes. Dropped one stone. That was all. I had no plans to build a dam, and I didn't get any benefit from having the water change course."

"You were playing god?"

"I was . . . playing."

It wasn't enough, but anything more would push Wade into making something up. Jericho took a moment to be sure he was really as calm as he felt, then toed his shoes off and stepped onto the sleeping bag.

"Shove over," he ordered.

"You think we're going to sleep here? Both of us? There's not a hell of a lot of room."

"I've slept in worse, and so have you."

Wade didn't argue any more, just slid over so there was enough space for most of Jericho to fit onto the thin mattress.

"Not ideal," Jericho admitted, shifting onto his side so he'd need less floor space.

Wade's face was inches from his. "Seems okay to me."

It wasn't the dream. They were nowhere tropical, and they sure didn't have the big mattress and the clean white sheets. But Wade looped his hand over Jericho's hip and pulled him in a bit tighter, then shifted and prodded with his head until he was using Jericho's arm as a pillow, and Jericho let his body relax.

"Yeah," Wade said. "This is good."

And they slept that way, close as they could be, while the sun rose and shone its light on a new day of life in Mosely, Montana.

CHAPTER 20

Jericho went home that morning, had a long shower, and fell into bed to get some of the sleep he'd missed the night before. He slept until late afternoon and thought about taking the rest of the day off. Even as a witness rather than a suspect, he'd be kept as far away from the Wooderson shooting case as possible, so there was no pressing need for him to be at work. But things weren't tidied up yet, and he didn't like that.

So he put on a fresh uniform and headed to the station. Kayla looked like she'd been up all night, but that wasn't too surprising, considering there'd been another damn murder in her jurisdiction.

"We found the kids at a friends' place, like you said," she told him. "And I called Detective Fernandez to let her know. She actually cried, she was so happy."

"I don't blame her."

Kayla nodded. "Pretty convenient, the way this worked out. The Applebys kicked things into gear fast, and Will's new lawyer has already been in touch. I expect we'll be cutting Will loose tonight or early tomorrow. With the FBI investigating Wooderson in this case as well as Ohio, the evidence against Will doesn't mean much. And it all could have been part of the frame-up. Hell, even the fingerprints on the two-by-four are *so* clear they're starting to look like an obvious plant. Wooderson must have handed the thing to Will, or maybe swung it at him, slow enough that Will would catch it, and then taken it away to bury where he knew it would be found." She shook her head. "This is turning into a happy ever after, practically."

"Lorraine's still dead. Will's still going to be fucked up from it all. I'd say it went from totally, irreversibly fucked to slightly, less-completely disastrous."

"Well, you're a glass-half-empty kind of guy," she said. Her lightness was a little forced, but he didn't call her on it. It was far from his place to tell her how she should deal with anything, let alone something like this.

"Yeah, I guess maybe I am."

"And you don't seem completely satisfied with this situation. I know you already answered a bunch of questions as a witness last night, but think like a cop, now. Help me figure this out. We have to assume Wooderson was killed because of this case, don't we? We'll look for other motives, obviously, but working theory? He was packing up to leave town, and somebody stopped him. Who knew enough about this case to know how serious it would be if he got away?"

It was a good question. Jericho wouldn't mention Fernandez's name, wouldn't cast suspicion on her when he knew it was unwarranted. But Kayla was staring at him, waiting for an answer. She squinted and said, "What do you know, Jay? What are you not telling me?"

Another good question, unfortunately. "I don't *know* anything," he said carefully. And even if he had known, he was pretty sure where his loyalties would lie, although much less certain of what that meant. "But, all the same, I typed up my resignation. I think I've come to the end of the line in this job."

"Why?" She didn't seem shocked, but it sounded like she really wanted to hear the answer. "If you know nothing about this case, why quit because of it?"

He stared out the window, looking at the summer-fresh landscape and the wild mountains beyond. "Because I think the killer was right. Because I don't want to catch him, or be part of a system that catches him. Not because of who he might be, but because . . . the system failed, Kay, and the guy who shot Wooderson? *He* didn't fail."

"You know the arguments about vigilantes." She frowned at him, waiting, then prompted, "The system is in place to protect the innocent. It's impossible to be sure about guilt without a fair trial. Justice should be based on logic and compassion, not anger and revenge."

"Yeah, I know the arguments. But in this case? The system wasn't protecting the innocent, because Wooderson was going to go kill another woman somewhere. And in this case? I'm damn sure about his guilt, trial or not. And, seriously, *in this case*? I think the shooter acted out of logic and compassion, not anger and revenge. I don't think he was trying to avenge a murder, I think he was trying to prevent another one. He did what had to be done to protect people."

"You've been a cop for almost a decade. You're going to throw it away over one case?"

"Looking back, though, it's *not* just one case. This one got under my skin a bit more, but there have been other times when I knew someone was guilty and couldn't do anything about it. Other times when that person probably went on to kill again. And I let it go. I tried not to think about it because there was nothing I could do. I shut the door and pretended it was a wall, but it never was, and the door is open now, and I don't think I should shut it again."

She frowned at him. Possibly that last metaphor had been a bit much, but he was pretty confident in his decision, overall. Confident enough that he didn't feel like it needed to be discussed, really. But she was his friend as well as his boss, so he waited. And finally she said, "So what's the alternative?"

"I'm not saying we should overthrow the system. I just think it's best if the people who work for it truly believe in it, you know?"

"I don't mean for the justice system, I mean for you. If you're not being a cop, what are you going to do?"

"I have no idea."

"*No* idea?" She leaned back in her chair. "No plans to go riding off into the sunset with a certain old friend? No schemes about shutting yourself away from the rest of the world and just being a big glob of romance for the rest of your life?"

Sometimes he wished she didn't know him quite so well. "I don't think I was planning to be a 'big glob' of anything. But, yeah, okay, maybe I was thinking of something along those lines. Would it be so bad?"

"It'd probably be great for a week or two. Assuming you could convince him to leave his current life, which doesn't seem like an automatic thing, to me. Just because you're having a big crisis of faith doesn't mean he is. But, okay, assume he went along with you. How long do you think you could do that for? How long before it starts creeping into your brain that you've abandoned a world that needs you? How long before your companion gets bored and pulls a Wade, messing everything up simply for the challenge of trying to fix it again? Jesus, Jay, think about it! The man is the *opposite* of laid-back. He's always got to have a plan, or seven, always got to be manipulating things and playing the angles. How long's it going to last, you and him in your peaceful new life? You're going to throw away your career for something that temporary?"

"This isn't about Wade. Not most of it. I'm quitting because I don't think I'm right for the job anymore. Why are you resisting this? I've been a pain in the ass since I got here. I mean, you suspended me not long ago—obviously you know I'm not an ideal cop!"

"You have been a pain in the ass," she agreed. "But you've also gotten things done. You saved the kids—and do I want to know how they fit into your escape plan? You going to walk away from them, leave them with Nikki?"

Just like he'd already let them down by not protecting them from Eli. Sure, he hadn't known they existed, but the *world* had needed to be protected from Eli, and Jericho hadn't done a thing about it. Jericho hadn't, but somebody else had. His brain stuttered over that for a moment. Someone had stopped Eli. Someone had taken care of what Jericho hadn't.

Kay seemed to think his distraction was a sign that she was gaining ground. "The biker situation was a mess in all ways—I can't say you solved anything, there, but neither did anyone else. This case? In this case, you're the one who realized there was something going on! If you hadn't been on the case we would have convicted Will Archer for murder, *and* Keith Wooderson would have gone on to kill again. I'm not saying any of it's tidy, or as clear as might be convenient, but, come on, buddy! You make a difference—you're helping people."

He dragged his mind back to the conversation. "I wonder how your dad justified it at the start." It felt like a low blow, but he hoped she knew him well enough to realize he didn't mean it that way. "Did he tell himself that he was helping people, so it wasn't really that big of a deal if he took some cash on the side? Wasn't hurting anyone to pass along a bit of information now and then, and why shouldn't he make a decent living for doing a tough damn job?" He paused long enough to make sure his voice was gentle when he asked, "You think that's how it went with him?"

His caution either worked or wasn't necessary, because she didn't flinch when she said, "That's a completely different situation. You start bending the rules for your own benefit? We'll have a problem. But bending the rules for the good of the community?"

"I'm condoning murder, Kay. It's well past bending the rules." It was breaking the laws of man. But maybe not the laws of Jericho.

"Condoning isn't the same as committing." She stopped and gave him a thoughtful look. "Wade. Wade shot Wooderson—to keep you from doing it. To keep you pure." Another pause, then, "Shit. That's— It's like you're the kid in that Terminator movie, with the high-power robot at your command."

"Have you ever in your life seen Wade Granger take a 'command'?"

Another pause. "You didn't even have to ask him. He just did it. Jesus, Jay, is that honestly what you want to sign up for? A pet psychopath? What if you come home from work one day and bitch about somebody—you going to be okay when that person turns up with a bullet in his brain?"

"Are we talking about Hockley? Because in his case . . ."

But Kayla obviously didn't want to joke about it. "Take some time off. Get out of town for a few days and, sure, if you can, take Granger with you, see what he's like in an atmosphere that's a little less blood-soaked and testosterone-baked. Settle down and think it all through. Then come back and make a decision when you've had enough sleep and aren't still seeing Wooderson's brains on the driveway."

"Why are you arguing with me on this? I mean, you honestly think I'm wrong?"

She shook her head impatiently. "I think you're overly dramatic. I think you're a pain in the ass. But I think you're a hell of a lot better than Jackson, so if I can't be here doing this job, you should be."

"Kay, they're not going to— What, you're worried they're going to try a recall? No, you're paranoid. News about your dad isn't even out yet, not fully. There are some rumors, maybe, but not enough to cause you any trouble."

She sighed and flopped back in her chair. "Jackson knows. So as soon as he's ready, as soon as he's got all his ducks in a row, he'll leak it, and the shit will fly. And, honestly, Jay, I'd be okay with it.

I could accept that maybe I don't deserve the job, not if I was so totally clueless about corruption going on right under my nose. I could go find another job, but not if it means Jackson taking over. I mean . . . he'd be terrible. The people deserve better than that, don't they?"

"I have no idea what anyone deserves." Not the town, not himself, not Wade, not Eli. He could feel the exhaustion creeping up on him. The clarity that had come with deciding to quit the force had buoyed him up, but now that the decision was being dissected, he could feel himself sinking. "I don't want to be a hypocrite. I don't want to be a bad cop."

"And the self-doubt you feel about all that may be part of what makes you a good cop," Kayla said gently. Then she added, "Or maybe you're a crooked bastard who's going to drag the department into even more disrepute. Who the hell knows?"

"Your pep talks are a bit bittersweet, you know that?"

"I've never been much for the pep." She pushed her chair away from the desk and stood up with energy that seemed only a little forced. "Take some time off. Get out of town. Come back refreshed and we'll see where everything stands. Sound good?"

He didn't want to agree. Everything would be so much easier if there was just one black-and-white boundary in his life, one bridge he could burn that didn't get rebuilt with scrap metal and rough, salvaged lumber. But apparently he wasn't going to get that clarity, not right then.

"Okay," he said grudgingly. "I'll take a break and get back to you."

"Thank you," she said. And he supposed that was enough.

Jericho should have waited. He was too tired, too strung out, too nerve-jangly and adrenalized to deal with anything complicated. It was absolutely not a great time to talk to Nikki. Still, he'd gone by the house on the way back to his apartment, and she'd been home. So.

"Eli was an asshole." It seemed meaningless, considering they both knew it perfectly well, but it had occurred to him that he'd never expressed the sentiment to Nikki's face. So he sat there on her secondhand couch, staring at her scowl, and said, "I have no idea why you married him and it's none of my business. But I want to say it, right now, for whatever record there is between you and me: Asshole. Abusive, angry son of a bitch."

She just sat there. Watching and waiting, and for a moment, Jericho felt as if maybe *he* was the asshole in all this, dragging up the past. But he thought of his reasons for coming over, and drew at least a little strength from them.

"He beat the shit out of me when I was a kid," he said. Strange how hard it still was to say the words. "Not my mom, usually, but sometimes her too, if he was really on a tear. He—" What? Jericho had never done the therapy thing, but he'd talked to people who had, heard all their jargon, all their pasted-on explanations for something that seemed a hell of a lot simpler on its own. Jericho didn't want to talk about how Eli hadn't been given any positive male role models or hadn't understood appropriate ways to express his frustration. "He was an asshole."

"But I married him," Nikki finally said. "I walked into it with my eyes open. I had kids with him." It sounded like a challenge, but Jericho could hear it differently, if he listened through his younger ears. Sometimes people needed answers to questions they couldn't ask.

So Jericho responded with, "Wade says Eli had a lot of good qualities. I didn't see many of them, from my perspective, but Wade's pretty smart, especially when it comes to understanding people. And he has some nice things to say about Eli."

"And you have some nice things to say about Wade," Nikki replied, clearly fighting to get a smirk back on her face.

But Jericho was too tired for that shit. "You married Eli, for whatever reasons. And for another set of reasons, reasons I think I understand better than the first, you killed him." Inexcusable that it had taken him so long to figure it out. Sexist, probably, assuming that a woman, even a woman like Nikki, couldn't have committed the crime. But once he'd gotten past whatever the mental barriers had been, it all made sense.

"There must have been a final straw. He'd been beating you for a while, I'm guessing. Maybe it started small and got worse. You've got no money, no family to run to, and you hate the cops way too much to trust them to help you. And you're tough. Proud. It must have been something serious that sent you to the shelter, but the woman there didn't mention you seeming banged up or needing medical care. So I'm thinking he hit one of the kids." It felt wrong to make this kind of a speech without giving her a chance to respond, but he needed to get it all out first, let her know his perspective, before she said anything that would set them down a path too narrow to turn around on.

"He pushed you too far, so you pushed him off the cliff. I think you had your damn bike in the back of the truck and rode it home along the trail—that's why the forensics lab only found one set of tire tracks going out there. Somehow Mike DeMonte knows about it—" That was what he'd meant when he'd told Jericho to look closer to home. Not Wade, but Nikki. "—and that's not good. He'll probably tell the feds anything he knows, eventually, in order to get a sweeter deal. And Wade knows." Which was why he'd told Jericho to let it all go and not keep poking. Because if Jericho could have lived the rest of his life without having this knowledge, everything would have been a hell of a lot easier. "And now I know."

"You don't know shit," she growled. "All you've got is guesses and theories."

"I know," he said, and he did. He might not have the evidence to prove it, but he knew it all the same. So for the second time in two days, he was faced with an unrepentant killer he couldn't convict.

But Nikki wasn't a thrill-killing psychopath. She'd had a reason for doing what she'd done, and there was no reason to believe she'd do it again. There was no one to protect, no future crimes to prevent.

So he said, "I'm okay with it. Not as a cop. Maybe not as his son. But as a man? Away from all the rest of it? I think I understand why you did it, and even if I don't understand, I'm willing to let it go. I'm *able* to let it go."

She narrowed her eyes into suspicious slits. "That's big of you. I mean, I'm not saying I did *shit*, but if I had? I wouldn't be looking for your forgiveness. You don't mean a goddamn thing to me."

And, yes, that was about where he should have expected the conversation to go. And maybe she was right—maybe his forgiveness and understanding was more about his own ego than anything else. But he didn't think that mattered, right then. He'd said his piece, cleared the air, and it was time to move on. "We need to make sure we understand each other," he said, and she just stared at him, waiting for the next shoe to drop.

"The easiest thing would be for me to walk away," he continued, and for a moment that option opened before him like a beautiful paradise, a world of calm and simplicity and peace. But then he felt the claws closing around his ankles, not scratching him—not yet—but pulling him back. Tugging, then yanking, increasingly insistent, increasingly desperate. Nikki, Elijah, Nicolette, Kayla, the sheriff's office, law enforcement as a whole.

It was strange to realize the one factor that wasn't tugging at him. It wasn't pulling because it didn't need to. Wherever he went, for the rest of his life, one element would always be with him, just as it always had been. And Jericho was fine with it. Wade was his, and he was Wade's, and the world wasn't allowed to get in the way of that ever again.

So he said, "Yeah, it would be easiest to leave. But I'm not going to, at least not right now." Not alone. "So you and I are still going to be in contact, and I want you to understand what I'm saying about Eli's death." He waited until she frowned at him, then he said, "I'm ready to believe he got what he deserved. Probably he deserved it a hell of a lot earlier than he got it. And I don't want his kids to suffer because they had a shitty father—not any more than they already have." Not any more than *he* already had, but he wasn't going to bring that up in front of Nikki. "So they need their mom, and they need her not in jail. You understand what I'm saying?"

She glared over his shoulder. "So you're not going to turn me in? Is that all this has been about?"

"For Eli's murder? No, I'm not going to tell anyone what I think happened. I'm going to let that go." He leaned in, tried to catch her eyes, then gave up and spoke to her stubborn, jutted-out chin. "But for all the rest of this shit? Running drugs for Wade, or whatever the hell else you're doing? That's on *you*, Nikki. I'll do what I can to protect you from anything related to Eli. But, no, I can't and I fucking *won't* cover for the rest of your shit. If you want to run drugs because you think it's better than waiting tables? That's not because of Eli, that's because of *you*, your mistake, and I'm not going to do a goddamn thing to keep you from feeling the consequences."

"So what's the point of all this, then?" she demanded.

"The point is you have two kids. I'm honestly not crazy about either of them, but they're my blood, and that seems to mean something to me. If you go to jail, they're fucked, and I don't care what line of goods Wade has sold you about taking care of them—Wade isn't suited to raise a goat, let alone a human child. I know, he can control them, but—" But what? Should Jericho get Freudian and start babbling about Wade raising the kids with pure Id? Letting the kids stay uncontrolled and vicious. No, that wouldn't go over well. "Wade is a short-term solution, if that. *You're* the long-term solution, and for that to work, you need to keep your ass out of jail."

Her expression didn't change. "You think I'm a shitty mother. The only reason you think I'd be better than Wade is some sexist bullshit about ovaries or something. You think any woman, even one you can't stand, would raise kids better than any man."

"No," he said, and he was pretty sure he meant it. "I think—I mean, I know it doesn't matter what I think, but since you brought it up—I think they could do with a little discipline, yeah. A bit of structure to their lives. Maybe a vegetable or two that doesn't come with cheese and a crispy crust. But overall? You love them, Nikki, and you're doing what you have to in order to protect them. I get that, and I respect it."

"But?" she spat, the word sharp and hard as a fragment of glass.

"But you're set up to go to jail. You're doing Wade's dirty work for him, and the feds are all over him, looking for weaknesses, and they're going to find you. So, the past? I'll do what I can to protect you from the past. But everything from— No, not everything from here on. Everything from *that day* on, everything from the day you pushed Eli over the damn cliff and watched him fall? That's on you, and I won't do a thing to protect you from any of it."

"I never asked you to," she growled.

"Bullshit. You dragged me back here to cover for you while you shopped that thumb drive around, you get me to babysit when actually I'm just giving you a cover story for whatever smuggling bullshit you're up to—don't tell me you haven't asked me to protect you."

Her smile was pure bravado, a façade of bravery when they both knew there was no substance beneath it. "So?" she demanded. "What's changing?"

"Maybe nothing." Yeah, he was too tired for all this. "I just—I wanted things to be clear between us. I wanted you to know what I was thinking."

"Because your thoughts are *so* valuable to the world," she said. "Fine. Now I know all about them. But if you don't have anything more important to talk about—" She stopped as if she was catching herself. Maybe remembering her larger strategy and all the ways it could be useful to have an under-sheriff on her side. Or maybe—just maybe—thinking of the ways it might be good to have a brother on her kids' side. "The kids are starting school next week. And Elijah still hasn't seen his snakes. You got a plan for that?"

"Not really," he confessed.

"Well, maybe you'd better get one."

He probably should. Hell, maybe he'd ask Wade for help. Maybe the two of them wouldn't run away to the beach together; maybe they'd take two feral children on a snake-hunting expedition instead.

"I'll figure something out," he promised. And he meant it. If he and Wade were working together? Hell, yeah. They'd make it work. Jericho would settle for nothing less.

Explore more of the *Common Law* series at:
riptidepublishing.com/titles/series/common-law

Dear Reader,

Thank you for reading Kate Sherwood's *Darkness*!

We know your time is precious and you have many, many entertainment options, so it means a lot that you've chosen to spend your time reading. We really hope you enjoyed it.

We'd be honored if you'd consider posting a review—good or bad—on sites like **Amazon, Barnes & Noble, Kobo, Goodreads, Twitter, Facebook, Tumblr,** and your blog or website. We'd also be honored if you told your friends and family about this book. Word of mouth is a book's lifeblood!

For more information on upcoming releases, author interviews, blog tours, contests, giveaways, and more, please sign up for our weekly, spam-free newsletter and visit us around the web:

Newsletter: tinyurl.com/RiptideSignup
Twitter: twitter.com/RiptideBooks
Facebook: facebook.com/RiptidePublishing
Goodreads: tinyurl.com/RiptideOnGoodreads
Tumblr: riptidepublishing.tumblr.com

Thank you so much for Reading the Rainbow!

RiptidePublishing.com

(all m/m – for m/f see Cate Cameron at catecameronauthor.com)

AUTHOR

Kate Sherwood started writing about the same time she got back on a horse after almost twenty years away from riding. She'd like to think she was too young for it to be a midlife crisis, but apparently she was ready for some changes!

Kate grew up near Toronto, Ontario, and went to school in Montreal, then Vancouver. But for the last decade or so she's been a country girl. Sure, she misses some of the conveniences of the city, but living close to nature makes up for those lacks. She's living in Ontario's "cottage country"—other people save up their time and come to spend their vacations in her neighborhood, but she gets to live there all year round!

Since her first book was published in 2010, she's kept herself busy with novels, novellas, and short stories in almost all the subgenres of m/m romance. Contemporary, suspense, sci-fi, or fantasy— the settings are just the backdrop for her characters to answer the important questions: How much can they share, and what do they need to keep? Can they bring themselves to trust someone, after being disappointed so many times? Are they brave enough to take a chance on love?

Kate's books balance drama with humor, angst with optimism. They feature strong, damaged men who fight themselves harder than they fight anyone else. And, wherever possible, there are animals: horses, dogs, cats ferrets, squirrels . . . sometimes it's easier to bond with a nonhuman, and most of Kate's men need all the help they can get.

With her writing, Kate is still learning, still stretching herself, and still enjoying what she does. She's looking forward to sharing a lot more stories in the future. (And check out her imaginary friend, Cate Cameron, who writes m/f romance and YA.)

You can find Kate at:

Facebook: facebook.com/kate.sherwood.79

Twitter: twitter.com/kate_sherwood

Goodreads: goodreads.com/author/show/3462951.Kate_Sherwood

Enjoy more stories like *Darkness* at RiptidePublishing.com!

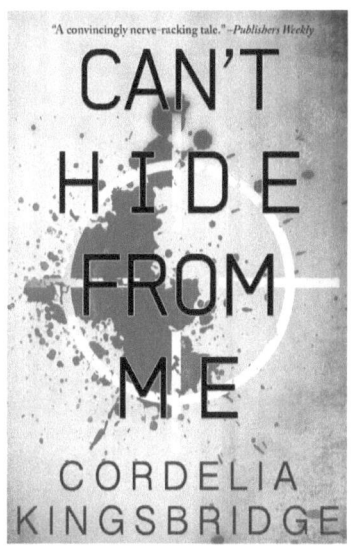